Bluebottle Poison

Also by Jude Murphy and published by Ginninderra Press
Scrapbooks and Broken Strings

Jude Murphy

Bluebottle Poison

Bluebottle Poison
ISBN 978 1 76109 526 9
Copyright © text Jude Murphy 2023
Cover image: Roxy Taylor

First published 2023 by
GINNINDERRA PRESS
PO Box 3461 Port Adelaide 5015
www.ginninderrapress.com.au

For Ashlie
If only…

Put the shells in my bucket and watch the waves
I'm wondering which kind of life God saves
Surely I'm much too close to the start
As blue-bottle poison is filling my heart
– Jude Murphy, 'In a Child's Mind'

1

My hand is on a teenage boy's crotch.

I'm squished in the back seat of the car. My sister, June, sits at the window. I'm next to her, sharing a seatbelt with my brother's friend Mitchell, who sits next to my brother, Cameron. Yes, it's all highly illegal, but it's the eighties and our maroon Valiant almost always carries more passengers than seat belts.

Mitchell has a sleeping bag on his lap, hiding his crotch from my brother. He's pulling my eleven-year-old hand onto the front of his satiny football shorts, jiggling it around, his face an enthusiastic grimace, encouraging me to keep it going. And I'm there, a stupid little girl, too shy to pull my hand away but too fearful to massage his fleshy bulge, simply laughing nervously and shaking my head, my arm draped across his sweaty thigh, all floppy, the hot wind blasting through the back window of the car flattening my hair to one side and roaring in my ears so that I can see my dad's lips moving as he sits behind the wheel of the car but I can't hear a word.

It's January. Australian summer. We're headed down the south coast to my aunt and uncle's dairy farm. At eleven years of age, there is nothing that excites me more than our annual trip to Aunty Ruby and Uncle Evan's dairy farm. At eleven years of age, I love to pretend that I own it. I mean, sure, the property is run by my aunty and uncle and there are always grown-ups around barking orders, but each time we've completed the mountainous descent and our Valiant rattles to a halt at the gate at the bottom of Aunty Ruby and Uncle Evan's gravel driveway, I feel like I've come home.

We reach the driveway. The car pulls up and my father calls out, 'Who's going to open the gate?'

Before anyone can beat me to it, I reach across and open the door, scrambling over June and running around the front of the car, unhooking the latch and hoisting myself up on the gate as it swings open. I can hear the working dogs, Jess and Bell, already barking, signalling our arrival, and Aunty Ruby is probably watching me from the kitchen window, ducking and weaving her head to make out my figure between the branches of the ancient Moreton Bay fig tree.

Dad moves the car forward and I latch the gate behind him. He takes off, singing out the window, 'We'll meet you up there.'

And I take off on foot, running up the hill, gravel crunching beneath my grubby sneakers. Already, when I lick my lips, I can taste the salt of the ocean behind the hill.

I try to beat the car up to the house. I want to be the first one to reach the back door, see Aunty Ruby and Uncle Evan, smell the real pine tree covered in Christmas ornaments in the lounge room. I want things to be the way they always are. I want things to be normal. I want the sickness in the pit of my gut to go away. I want the feeling of Mitchell's crotch that still burns the palm of my hand to disappear. I want everyone to talk and laugh and I want to look at all their faces and make sure that none of them know, that none of them can see my shame.

But, as usual, I don't beat the car. By the time I reach the top of the driveway, breathless and sweaty, everyone is already standing around, saying hello and shaking hands. Mum introduces Mitchell to my aunty and uncle and he smiles and says hello and acts all polite and I wish he would hop back in the car and take off down the driveway and I would never have to see him again. I try to avoid eye contact but when I do find the courage to glance at him he's looking straight at me, smirking, and it feels like now we share a secret that I wish I didn't know.

I move towards Uncle Evan, say hello.

He's wearing dark blue dungarees and a blue, checked flannelette shirt, rolled up at the sleeves, exposing his forearms, thick from years of milking. He wraps me in a bear hug and scolds in a harsh tone,

'What have I told you about swinging on that gate, young Bridie? If it comes off its hinges, it's you who'll be fixing it!'

I give him a smile. He always says this, and after all the times I've swung on the gate it hasn't come off its hinges once.

I say hello to Aunty Ruby and give her a hug as she brushes her lips against my cheek. She's dressed in khaki shorts and a black singlet, her hair pinned up as the south coast breeze blows wispy strands across her face. There's a smoky grey cat circling around her feet.

'Look at you!' she cries. 'We'll need to put a brick on your head if you get any bloody taller, Bridie. What's your mother been feeding you?'

Dad lights a cigarette, hangs it out the side of his mouth while he lifts the suitcases out of the boot of the car. Aunty Ruby tells everyone to come inside. She tells us there's tea and sponge cake. We follow her in and see she's already put a pot of tea in the middle of the long dining room table, snuggled into one of her home-made, crocheted tea cosies. She goes into the kitchen and returns with the cake on a plastic plate. She lays a knife and a pile of saucers next to the cake and normally I'd be the first one to wolf into a slice, but today my stomach hurts. I can still feel Mitchell's crotch in my hand and the thought of it makes me feel a bit sick.

Mum takes a seat at the table. Her and Aunty Ruby talk about the trip down. Mum tells her there was quite a bit a traffic and complains that she wishes they would widen the roads. Aunty Ruby assures her that this is 'on the cards' and tuts in sympathy for the businesses who 'won't stand a chance'.

I watch June crawl into Mum's lap and Mum gently runs her fingers through June's silky black bob cut. Dad is carrying suitcases down the hall into the spare bedrooms where we'll be sleeping, and Uncle Evan is showing Cameron and Mitchell one of his new rifles. The boys are already making plans to go spotlighting. It's noisy and close here in the dining room, and when Dad returns and Uncle Evan offers him a cold tinny, I quietly back up and slip out the back door.

I breathe in, a huge gulp of south coast cool, and take a look around. I have so many favourite places on my aunt and uncle's farm that it's hard to decide in which direction I should walk. I look out over the house paddock and see lush, green pasture dotted with grazing Friesian cows, all the way down to the dam. Behind them, I see the huge hill that makes up most of the property. It's so tall that the top of it seems to brush the sky, and it's covered in clumps of dense scrub. The ocean is there, behind that hill. I know this because my brother and my cousins have walked over that hill and have swum in the ocean and walked back again and have told me all about it. But I've never been allowed.

If I step up onto the veranda and follow it round to the other side of the house, I will find the enormous Moreton Bay fig tree, its trunk so thick it would take my whole family to link arms around it. I love to climb the tree, and a number of times I've scaled it right to the top and I've crawled out to the edge of a high bough and have gotten stuck, calling out for my dad or Uncle Evan, who have had to come rescue me and bring me back down again, telling me off and calling me a dumb cat.

If I follow the footpath, I will pass the stinking outhouse and come across the dogs – border collies, Jess and Bell. They're chained to their star pickets, lying in their kennels, a couple of halved forty-four-gallon drums. I will pat them and they'll pant and wag their tails and lie on their backs with their legs sprawled, inviting me to scratch their tummies. If I want to do this, I need to act fast. If Uncle Evan sees me patting the dogs, there'll be hell to pay. 'You'll ruin those bloody dogs patting them!' he'll yell. 'They're not bloody pets!'

Behind the dogs is the chook house. As I approach, I hear the long, scraping chatter of the chooks, their heads bobbing forwards and backwards as they step about. During the day, the chooks are loose, free to circle the house and scratch in the dirt. In the evening, Uncle Evan or Aunty Ruby will chase them with the plastic rake that's leaning up against the chook house, hunting them into their large cage with its wooden plank that leads up into the straw-lined box where the chooks sleep at night, protected from the foxes. In the morning, they'll leave fresh, warm eggs that Uncle Evan will collect after the morning milking. Uncle Evan will try to get me to stick my hands underneath the nesting chooks and feel for eggs, and I will try, yet again, to slide my hand beneath their smooth feathery breasts, but at the last moment I'll rip my arm back, too scared of getting pecked.

I walk past the chook house. After looking around, in the end I settle on the one place I want to see more than anything else. My favourite place. The milking shed. I walk across the spongy grass and arrive at the shed door. I lift the little piece of rope that opens a latch on the other side of the door, and I go in.

I see the huge silver vat that holds the milk after each milking session. I imagine it swirling around, a chalky whirlpool. I move inside the shed and see the stalls where every morning and evening Uncle Evan's dairy cows stand, lazily munching on pollard and bran as the milk is drawn from each udder. Uncle Evan uses machinery these days instead of hand-milking, but whenever we visit, I always ask him to milk one of the heifers by hand. I love to hear the spurt of the milk drumming against the bottom of the bucket. My senses feast on the smells: cow dung, lucerne hay and well-oiled leather. And today, there's something else I'm not expecting. The unmistakable scent of horse. I'm immediately intrigued. As far as I know, Uncle Evan doesn't have a horse.

I move through the dairy shed and round the corner where I see, standing there in the small holding yard, the most magnificent creature I've ever seen. He's a thoroughbred, tall as a racehorse. His coat is a satiny liver chestnut. Chocolate eyes. I see his muscled rump, sloped at an angle as he rests his left hind leg. He notes my arrival with a sharp lift of the head and a soft nicker. I instinctively click my tongue and he wanders over, stretching his neck through the yard rail. He's searching for a treat, but my hands are empty. I stroke his velvety muzzle and bury my nose in his ear. Drinking him in. I'm wondering how Uncle Evan could have failed to tell me he has a horse.

'What are you doing, Bridie?'

I jump. June's only seven years old and I'm shocked that she's been able to open the milking shed door by herself.

'What are you doing here?' I ask her.

'Mum told me to come and find you.'

'Go back to the house.'

She ignores me, looks beyond me and takes in the horse. 'Wow,' she whispers. She makes a move to pat the horse, but I slap her outstretched arm and she cries out, snatching her arm back and holding it with her other hand. 'What did you do that for?'

'You can't pat him,' I tell her. 'He might bite you.' I'm not happy that June is here. I don't want her ruining this moment. I don't want to see that the horse is just as friendly with June as he is with me.

June's face crumples and fat tears spill from her eyes. 'I'm telling,' she threatens.

This isn't good. Any form of conflict between me and June never ends well for me.

'June,' I say. 'I'm sorry. I'm so sorry. Of course you can pat him.'

She eyes me sceptically.

'I only tried to stop you because I don't want you to get hurt. But I'm sure that if I'm here he won't hurt you.'

June steps forward. The tears stop and her face relaxes as she cautiously stretches her arm out to pat the horse's head. He snorts loudly and nudges her hand, looking again for a treat.

'See…when a horse does that, it means he really likes you,' I inform her. I'm still in damage control.

'What's his name?' she asks me.

'Rocket,' I reply. I don't know where the name comes from but as soon as I say it, I'm convinced that this horse should be named Rocket.

'How do you know that?' She's not so easily fooled.

'Well,' I begin, 'if his name isn't Rocket then it should be. Why don't we say that Rocket is our special name for him, just for you and me?'

She likes the conspiratorial sound of this. 'Hello, Rocket,' she coos, moving closer.

I look down and note that she's wearing thongs, her unprotected toes dangerously close to Rocket's enormous hooves.

'Be careful, June. You don't want him stepping on your feet.'

She takes a step back. And I want to get her out of there, away from Rocket, my Rocket, and out of my milking shed.

'Come on,' I say. 'Let's go climb the fig tree.' And I walk her out of the shed, up on to the rickety veranda and around to the other side of the house.

*

In the afternoon, I ask Uncle Evan about the horse. But he warns me sternly, 'You stay clear of that horse, Bridie. That's Beau.'

'Bow?' I say. 'That's a weird name. Like a bow tie?'

'No, B-E-A-U. It's sort of a word that means…a handsome fella.'

'Oh. When did you get him?'

'He's not our horse. He's on agistment.'

'What does that mean?'

'It means he's a very, very expensive show horse and you're not to go anywhere near him. He belongs to a girl named Chelsea.'

My shoulders sag.

'Anyway,' he says, 'how come you haven't gone to visit Samantha yet? I'm sure she'll be home.'

Samantha lives with her mother in a house that is on my aunty and uncle's property but is about a hundred metres from their house. She's thirteen, a couple of years older than me. I'm only just going into Year 6 this year, but she's already done a year of high school. Samantha has lived in the house down the dirt road for as long as I can remember. We always play together, whenever we come down the coast for our yearly holiday. Last year, I even had a sleepover with her and we stayed up late watching television and flicking through her Dolly and Smash Hits magazines.

Uncle Evan's suggestion is a good one. I decide I'll go and visit Samantha.

June makes a big fuss. Cameron and Mitchell have gone for a walk, down to the dam and over the hill to visit the ocean. All the grown-ups are sitting around the table. Dad and Uncle Evan are nursing tinnies and Mum and Aunty Ruby are drinking peach-coloured bubbles out of tall wine glasses. June wants to come and visit Samantha with me. Of course, I don't want her tagging along. Samantha is my friend, not hers.

June starts carrying on, crying and whining about having no one to play with. In the past she's been too young to come with me on my visits to Samantha's, but Mum tells me she's older now, and eventually I'm given the ultimatum. If I want to visit Samantha, I have to take her with me.

We head off up the dirt track towards Samantha's house. I'm marching fast, striding my long legs and swinging my arms so that June has to run to keep up with me.

'Wait for me!' she pants.

'If you can't keep up, why don't you just stay behind?' I call back at her.

'That's not fair. Mum said you have to take me with you.' She's out of breath and it's an effort to get the words out.

I ignore her and start thinking about how excited Samantha will be to see me.

We arrive at Samantha's house. Her mother rents the house from Aunty Ruby and Uncle Evan, and like their house, Samantha's is really old. The outside is a pale blue colour with paint peeling off everywhere. I count about a dozen roof tiles that are missing and a veranda wraps around the right half of the house that has a couple of holes where the wooden floorboards have fallen through. I open the front gate, walk up the cracked concrete path and knock on the door. I ready my expression and prepare myself for Samantha's excited face when she sees me. So I'm a little bewildered when it's a boy who opens the door.

The boy is about Samantha's age, I guess, or maybe a bit older. He's tall and solid and sports the sandy locks and year-round tan of a surfie.

He looks really comfortable standing there in the doorway and I must look confused as I stand there with a stupid grin on my face because he tilts his head to the side like a curious puppy and says, 'Can I help you?'

'Um,' I stammer, 'I'm Bridie. I'm Samantha's best friend.' I've never actually asked Samantha whether I'm her 'best' friend. The word 'best' just sort of slips out. But it sounds good to say it.

He does a double-take and looks me up and down and then he calls out down the hall. 'Hey, Sammy! There's a kid here to see you!'

He takes a step back and I can see a shadow at the end of the hall.

'Hey, Samantha,' I sing out, because her name is Samantha, not Sammy, and I suppose this boy mustn't know her very well.

Samantha walks up the hall to the front door. She looks surprised and, I have to admit, not quite as delighted as I thought she'd be. When she doesn't say anything, I feel a bit awkward there and now June has moved right up behind me and is almost treading on my heels, tugging on the back of my shirt.

'It's Bridie,' I say.

'Oh, hey,' she says. And stands there.

It feels a bit strange. Normally, Samantha grins and gives me a big hug and her mother is usually standing behind her and she asks me inside, so I look over Samantha's shoulder to see if her mother is in fact there, about to ask me inside, but there's no one there and then the boy, the one who called her 'Sammy', swings an arm around Samantha's shoulder and Samantha sort of snuggles into his hip and puts one hand on his wide chest, right on top of the 'illa' on his Billabong T-shirt and I suddenly get the feeling that I won't be playing with Samantha this afternoon.

'We're here on our holiday,' I say stupidly.

'Um,' Samantha says, 'OK.'

Still, I just stand there, and I can feel June poking her head around me and in the corner of my eye I see her looking up at Samantha expectantly.

'Well, this is Dean,' she finally says, and Dean gives me a little wave, 'and we're doing some schoolwork together.'

Now I'm really confused. School doesn't start back for another month. What schoolwork could she possibly have to do?

'So I can't really have visitors right now. You'll have to go back home. Sorry.'

And still I stand there. I suppose I'm a little shocked and I can't seem to make myself speak. Or move. I see Samantha look up at the boy, Dean, and she rolls her eyes and he laughs a little and shakes his head and the door closes and I'm just standing there looking at the wood grain on the door and June is pressed up against my back.

'Let's go,' June says, taking my hand and pulling me down the concrete footpath and through the gate and we start walking back along the dirt track.

I walk a little way, slowly, and I'm looking down at the dirt and suddenly I feel in my right hand the satiny sheen of Mitchell's football shorts. I remember how awful it felt when he pulled at my hand and my throat gets all tight and tears fill my eyes and I can't see anything. And I stop there, in the middle of the track, and Samantha is probably watching me out the window, her and the stupid boy who doesn't even know her name, and an enormous sob escapes me so violently that I hear June gasp and then she moves in close and wraps both of her arms around my hips and she says, 'It's OK Bridie, It's OK,' the way I saw my mum comfort June once when she knocked her head on the underside of the dining room table.

'It's OK,' she says again.

And after a little while I calm down and we walk back up the dirt track in silence and by the time we get back to Aunty Ruby and Uncle Evan's house and the grown-ups ask us why we're back so early I tell them, 'There was nobody home.'

And June doesn't say a word.

2

The afternoon is hot and June and I want to go to the beach for a swim. But the grown-ups are settled in. They all sit around the dining room table, laughing and talking. Uncle Evan and Dad keep cracking the ring pulls on their blue-coloured beer cans, rotating them into stubbie holders. Mum and Aunty Ruby have refilled their wine glasses. It's clear we're not going anywhere this afternoon. June and I suggest we open the presents for us from Uncle Evan and Aunty Ruby that are under the Christmas tree, but we're reminded that Cameron and Mitchell are still on the other side of the hill and won't be back for hours and we're told to wait. At the sound of his name, Mitchell, my tummy does a little flip flop.

It's obvious I'm stuck with June. We head off to roam the house, leaving the grown-ups in the dining room.

I love the space in Uncle Evan and Aunty Ruby's house. The ceilings are high and the rooms are huge. In the morning, when the house has been closed up, it smells old. Musty. Like Dad's car when someone has left the windows down in a storm. But there are lots of windows and doors in the house that Aunty Ruby keeps open throughout the day. On a summer afternoon like this one, the breeze of the ocean is floating through, fresh and cool, and there's more than a hint of Christmas pine tree in the air. In the lounge room, real pine nettles have moulted from the tree's branches and have showered our wrapped gifts.

June and I quietly hunt around in the pile of presents looking for the ones with our names on the tags, careful not to make too much noise. We know we'll be scolded for poking and shaking presents. We find ours, both of them wrapped up in silver paper with white stars and bells. We squeeze them and rattle them. June's present is bigger than mine. It's an odd shape and the paper has been pulled over it awkwardly. Some bits are hard but the middle is soft. Mine is more of a square-shape and is also soft and hard in different places. But no matter how long we turn over our presents and massage their contents, we're no closer to guessing what they are.

We wander up the long hallway. I love standing at the top of Aunty Ruby and Uncle Evan's hallway. Two huge bedrooms sit off either side of it and at the end of the hallway is a wide door. When it's open like this, I can see the grassy pasture slope down away from the house and climb up again to the property's fence line. On the other side of the fence is the highway, the one that brought us here. The one that will take us home again.

On the walls of the hallway are pictures and photos. I know all of them so well I could draw a map of them without even looking. There's a timber-framed painting of a sailboat that my mum and dad brought back for Uncle Evan and Aunty Ruby when they went on a holiday to Queensland. There's a tapestry of a deer and its baby fawn, mounted in a silver frame. And there are photos. So many photos.

There's a wedding photo of Uncle Evan and Aunty Ruby. It's in colour, but not like the coloured photos that are taken with Mum's camera. The colours look almost like watercolour, as though they've been brushed in after the photo was developed. Uncle Evan is tall and slim with a full head of hair. But I know it's him. The eyes are still the same. Aunty Ruby wears a plain white dress with a neckline that plunges almost down to her belly button so you can see the curve of her breasts on either side. Her thick, dark curls are swept up in a nest on top of her head and a sparkly tiara sits at the front of it. Her cheeks are pink, her full lips ruby red.

There are photos of Uncle Evan and Aunty Ruby's children, our cousins. They're grown-ups now, but there are photos of them when they were as old as June and I are now. A school photo of their eldest boy, Peter, shows a freckly blond with a beaming smile, flashing his crooked teeth. Another photo is of Debbie, who is a few years younger than Peter. She wears long plaits that sit behind her ears and over the front of her shoulders, thick blue ribbons tied at the end of each one to match her blue checked school uniform. I only know this is Debbie because Aunty Ruby has told me. She doesn't look anything like my cousin Debbie does now. These days the family calls Debbie a 'fashion victim', but I love the way she looks. She has short-cropped, dyed blonde hair and wears lots of eye make-up. She dresses like Madonna, in short denim skirts and netted gloves on her hands. Huge, hooped earrings usually hang from her ears.

Debbie has two children. It's been explained to me that her two boys, Callum and Alex, are my second cousins, but we just call them our cousins. Callum is three. And her new baby Alex is just a few weeks old, born not long before Christmas.

There are more photos. Photos of Mum and Dad in a fancy restaurant, Mum drinking from a glass with a slice of pineapple and a spotted umbrella sticking out the top. There are photos of me and Cameron at the blowhole, before June was born. There's another photo of all three of us, Cameron in a navy suit, me in a lemon dress and June, just a baby, laughing at the camera with a gummy smile.

After looking at the photos, we wander into each bedroom. The first one on the left is where Cameron and Mitchell will be sleeping. There are three single beds and Dad has placed the boys' suitcases on the third bed. There are lots of pieces of furniture in the room. A dressing table, a large, timber-framed mirror on the wall, and a tall, deep cupboard that reminds me of a book we read at school, *The Lion, the Witch and the Wardrobe*. A couple of times, when I was younger, I crawled in and shut the door, convinced that if I waited long enough, a cavity at the back of the cupboard would reveal some secret world. Of course, it never did. Instead, I just sat uncomfortably amongst the winter jackets and pairs of boots that were crammed in there. Despite that, the cupboard does make an excellent hiding place.

The next bedroom is on the right of the hallway. Aunty Ruby and Uncle Evan's bedroom. We've always been told that this room is off limits. On occasion, I've snuck my head around the corner for a quick peek. I know that my uncle and aunty sleep in an old-fashioned, four-poster bed. The wood is deep red and glossy. There's a dressing table with a square mirror and little black handles on each of the drawers. There's a built-in cupboard in this room that has a wall-to-wall mirror. But I've never actually set foot inside this room.

Up at the end of the hall, the bedroom on the right is Mum and Dad's room. Their room has a double bed and a single bed. The rest of the suitcases are sitting on the single bed and Dad's wallet is already on the little bedside table. Through their bedroom window I can see the dam and the big hill that leads over to the ocean.

June and I will sleep, like we always do, in the enormous double bed in the room at the very end of the hall. The bed is so high off the ground that when I sit on it and dangle my legs, they don't even brush the floor. The ceilings are way high and the light switch isn't a flick switch like we have at home. Instead, it's a long piece of string hanging from the ceiling. To turn the light on and off, you have to pull on it until it clicks. When I lie in bed at night and look outside the window I can make out the headlights of distant cars crawling along the highway like a line of ants. And best of all, right outside the window, even when I'm lying in bed, I can see the fig tree.

We wander back outside through the open door at the end of the hallway. We turn right and follow the veranda around to the other side of the house until we come to another one of my favourite places on the farm: the sunroom. The sunroom is really just a dusty old box that has been tacked on to the side of the house, a bit like a storeroom. But in the sunroom is a piano.

It's not a great piano. It's not even a good piano. It's old and dusty and filled with spiderwebs and often when you strike a key, you're met with a mute thud. Uncle Evan and Aunty June refer to the piano as a 'pile of firewood'. But I love to sit and play it, plucking out little tunes using the notes that are available to me. I can spend hours here, imagining I'm performing for a hall full of people, or pretending to be a girl in some romantic painting, wearing a flowing white dress and playing pretty lullabies while a fat cat drapes itself lazily over the top of the instrument. And one of the best things about the piano is that June pays it no interest at all, so I never have to share it.

But June doesn't want to sit around watching me play the piano. She bugs me to leave, so we exit the sunroom and continue rounding the house. We come to the back door. We can see the grown-ups through the row of lead-light windows, laughing and talking, nursing their drinks. I contemplate going back inside, but then a splash of grey darts across the concrete footpath. June and I both gasp.

'A kitten!' she cries.

We both give chase, following the little grey bundle, cornering the house just in time to see its whip of a tail scurry into a tiny hole and disappear under the house.

We're both down on our hands and knees, peering into the hole that just swallowed the kitten. It's dark in there. And cool. And at first I can't see anything. But when my eyes adjust, I can make out a pair of glowing eyes, and then another, and another. I count three kittens in total, all pressed up together against a wooden plank. I judge that they're just within reach, but when I try to poke my arm through, I find the hole is too narrow. I ball my hand into a fist and then stretch the palm out flat, attacking the hole from all angles, but it's no good.

'June,' I say, 'you'll have to reach in there and get them out.'

June looks at me dubiously. This doesn't happen often, me moving aside to let June do something, but I have no choice. Only June's hand will fit. I reach out and grab her hand, guiding it towards the hole. She's resisting, pulling her hand back, but I hold it firmly.

'You have to,' I say. 'My hand won't fit. You do want to hold the kitten, don't you?'

With great hesitation, June bends her body, bringing her face down low and bringing her hand to the hole. Slowly, cautiously, she snakes her hand into the gap. It gets stuck and she needs to wriggle it around a little, but finally it pops through. I'm peering through a crack in the boards and start guiding her towards the kitten on the outside of the huddle of kittens, who shrinks back into its siblings at the sight of June's impending hand.

'You're nearly there,' I tell her. 'A little over this way. Almost…'

The kittens are pushed right up against the wooden plank now, but June connects with one of their tiny paws.

'That's it!' I yell. 'You've got it!'

And then the kitten swipes. June's hand recoils and she cries out, 'Ouch!' She's trying to rip her hand back into her body but the hand is stuck. She's panicking because she can't get her hand through and she's scared the kitten will scratch her again, so she's banging her hand against the other side of the hole. She's crying now, a frightened cry, and I'm trying to tell her to calm down, slow down, stop yanking her hand. She looks at me, her scared eyes wild.

'June,' I say, my hand on her shoulder. 'Stop struggling.'

And she does. She's still crying but she's still, and I hold her wrist gently and twist it around a little, pulling the fleshy heel of her palm and then her five fingers back out through the hole. She instantly clutches at her hand and I can see the scratch is deep, all the way across the back of her hand. It's bleeding and June is nursing her hand, rocking back and forth.

'June,' I say. 'Show me.'

Already she's getting up, ready to run inside, run to Mum, but I stand up in front of her, blocking her path.

'June!' I say. Louder now. Firmer. 'Show me the scratch.'

And she does. June shows me the scratch and her hand is shaking. But I order her to come with me and I take her over to the tap that's near the dogs' water bowl and I run it under the water.

'It's OK, June,' I tell her. 'There you go. It's all clean now. It's OK.'

When June has settled down, I lead her back over to the veranda. We sit for a while on the concrete steps and watch the cars crawl along the highway. Soon we come up with a game of pretend, singing songs and making up dance moves as though the veranda is our stage, each of us taking a turn to sit on the grass and be the audience.

When it's almost evening, Cameron and Mitchell emerge, trekking their way back down the hill. At the sight of Mitchell, a wave of sickness travels the length of my body, and I take June inside, where Mum and Aunty Ruby are cooking sausages for dinner.

When Uncle Evan sees us, he asks, 'So, have you found the kittens yet?' a cheeky smile on his face.

I look at June, expecting her to say we have, but she hides her scratched hand behind her back and shakes her head.

Uncle Evan simply nods. But something tells me he knows very well we found the kittens.

*

After dinner, we're finally allowed to open our presents. Cameron opens his little square gift and discovers a Rubik's cube. His first instinct is to complain that he already has one, but Dad tells him not to be 'such an ungrateful bastard' and he drops his head and mutters a 'thank you' to Aunty Ruby and Uncle Evan.

June's present is much better. She gets a snuggle pillow of a horse and there's a light in the middle and when you turn it on in a dark room it projects a circle of little horses onto the ceiling.

I open my present last. The soft thing I felt earlier is actually a beach towel, and the hard thing is a book with a picture of a girl swinging on a tree tyre on the front that looks really boring. I know better than to voice my disappointment so I smile at Aunty Ruby and tell her 'thank you' but deep down, I hate my present. I look across at June, clutching her horsey snuggle pillow and my envy pangs. I wish I got a horsey snuggle pillow.

At bedtime, June crawls into bed first and sleeps closest to the window. She tells me to pull on the cord that switches off the light and she hits the button on her snuggle pillow and a carousel of prancing horses start circling on the ceiling. The light glows bright then dull, bright then dull, melodic in its rhythm. It's beautiful, mesmerising.

But it's not mine. I don't want to watch the dancing horses. I close my eyes, roll over and go to sleep.

3

The rooster wakes me even before daylight can cast a shadow in the room. I'm not happy to be awake because as soon as I wake up, I always need to go to the toilet. Instantly. And to get to the toilet I have to pick my way across the bedroom and down the long, dark hallway, through the dining room, out the back door and along the concrete footpath to the outhouse.

The outhouse is the only thing I hate about Aunty Ruby and Uncle Evan's farm, but I know better than to say anything because the one time I told Aunty Ruby that the outhouse was disgusting and I asked her why she didn't have a flush toilet in the bathroom inside the house like everybody else, I got in big trouble. Mum told me off for being rude and I wasn't allowed to have any of Aunty Ruby's trifle for dessert and I had to do the dishes all by myself.

But there's no getting around it. I need to go to the toilet and I need to go now. I pad my way across the room and down the hall, past the dining room table and through the back door. And there, lying across the concrete footpath that leads to the outhouse is a big, horny bull.

I reel back in horror and shut the door. I pull the curtain aside and peer out the window. The bull is looking towards the door but he's not moving. He's not getting up. He's not going anywhere.

Now I really, really need to pee. I'm hopping up and down and I'm scared that soon I'm going to have an accident right there in my pyjamas. I cut back through the dining room and go back up the hallway and go into the room where Cameron and Mitchell are sleeping.

'Cameron!' I whisper as loudly as I can. 'Cameron!'

Cameron stirs. 'What?' he mumbles.

'There's a big bull at the back door and I have to go to the toilet.'

He lifts his head a little from the pillow. 'Just walk around it,' he instructs, and his head drops back on the pillow.

'No, Cameron, you have to go and shoo him away for me.' I shake his shoulder a little and then he gets really angry.

'Piss off!' he yells.

I start to move off and then I hear Mitchell speaking softly from the other bed. 'Bridie,' he says. 'I'll do it.'

I'm not at all happy with this turn of events. I aim to avoid interacting with Mitchell at all costs but it seems now I have no choice but to let him help me. He swings his legs over the side of the bed, has a bit of a stretch and a big yawn, and then he walks down the hall and out the door to the bull. He starts waving his arms around and the bull, surprised, thrusts his front legs out straight and uses his enormous hindquarters to awkwardly hoist himself up. He stands there, just staring at Mitchell, and I'm sure that I'm about to witness this bull murdering my brother's friend and I'm terrified but Mitchell lifts his arms above his head and yells out, 'Go on, get out of it!' and sort of stamps his foot a couple of times and the bull ducks his head and paws the ground but Mitchell holds firm and keeps waving his arms and stamping his foot and finally the bull swings around and takes off behind the fig tree.

'Thank you,' I mumble, and when he turns around to look at me, his eyes move up and down and he gets a funny look on his face and I'm suddenly conscious of my tiny pyjama shorts and my bare legs. That sick feeling from yesterday starts to rise up in my belly and I feel so warm inside my underpants that for a moment I think I really have had an accident.

'That's OK,' he says. He walks past me and pats me softly on the head.

I flinch at his touch and I pick up the pace, trotting away from him and into the outhouse, where I only just make it to the toilet in time.

When I return to the house, I'm met by Uncle Evan in the hallway. 'You're up then,' he says to me. 'You got your milking boots on?'

Uncle Evan waits for me to get dressed and we head out the back door. The sickness is still there a bit, but I feel a little better knowing Uncle Evan is here. He lets Jess and Bell off their chains and they run rings around him, yapping excitedly and swinging their tails. We walk over to the open shed that houses Uncle Evan's quad bike. With me on the back and the dogs trailing behind, we drive out across the paddock and round up the cattle. They wander into the milking shed easily. They're familiar with the milking. They do this twice a day, their udders swollen and leaking. Uncle Evan has tried to assure me that milking doesn't hurt them but they always look so uncomfortable, their back legs hooking widely, their full bags of milk swinging from side to side.

When we're back at the dairy shed, I can see Rocket, or Beau, in his holding yard. I don't go near the horse. Instead, Uncle Evan gets me to fill each cattle crush with pollard and bran. I love the smell and can't resist dipping my wet finger in the bucket and tasting it. Each cow wanders in easily and lowers her head, munching on breakfast and barely noticing the metal suckers Uncle Evan attaches to each teat. Some are so relaxed they lift their tails and drop a pile of steaming muck on the dairy floor for Uncle Evan to hose down later.

When the last cow comes into the shed, Uncle Evan brings out a couple of stainless-steel buckets. He upends one and takes a seat, placing the other bucket underneath the cow's udders. With his head resting on the warm belly of the cow, he starts massaging the cow's udder and squeezing on the teats. It takes a couple of tugs and then the milk shoots out in long spurts, one then the other, one then the other. After about a minute, he tells me it's my turn, and I take a seat, grab the teats with my small hands and start to pull. Nothing happens at first; it takes a while to remember how to use my thumbs to massage the milk out of the teat. I'm not as good as Uncle Evan, but I manage to get a little milk in the bucket.

After a while, Uncle Evan moves the bucket and attaches the metal suckers to the last cow. He whistles for Jess and Bell and lets them lap the contents of the bucket, their tails wagging like a couple of potty lambs. Then he takes me into the separate room where the milk enters the big stainless-steel vat. I watch the metal lever moving, swirling the milk. It's so smooth it looks solid, like you could reach out and stroke its surface.

When all the milking is done and Uncle Evan has hosed out the shed, the sun has started climbing the sky and Uncle Evan parks the quad bike and puts Jess and Bell back on their chains.

'Ready for some breakfast?' he asks.

I tell Uncle Evan that I'm hungry, but then we both notice a car at the bottom of the driveway. A girl gets out of the passenger side and opens the gate.

'Who's that?' I ask Uncle Evan.

'That's Chelsea. She'll be here to visit the horse.'

We stand there together, watching the car climbing up the driveway and parking close to the dairy shed.

Chelsea and an older woman get out of the car.

Uncle Evan calls out to them. 'Hi, Sondra. Chelsea.'

Sondra, who I assume is Chelsea's mother, smiles and waves.

'Hey there, Evan,' she replies, but Chelsea walks straight over to the dairy shed without saying a word.

Sondra moves to the boot of the car and unloads a shiny saddle and bridle as well as a soft bag that looks to be full of brushes.

Uncle Evan looks at me. I don't need to say a word. He knows how desperately I want to watch Rocket-Beau trotting around the round yard.

'C'mon, Bridie,' he says. 'Let's go have some breakfast.'

'Uncle Evan, please…please can I go watch the horse?' I can see by his tight grin that he's not keen. 'Pleeease?'

He turns back towards the visitors. 'Ah, hey, Sondra,' he calls out, straightening up his belt. 'This is my niece, Bridie.'

'Hello, Bridie,' she says as she struggles with her load.

'Any chance Bridie could watch Chelsea ride this morning? Of course, she'll stay right out of your way.'

'Sure,' says Sondra.

I squeal a little and give Uncle Evan a quick hug. Then I'm running to help Sondra with the tack. She thanks me and hands me a bridle, the leather reins soft in my hands, and I lift them to my nose and inhale deeply.

She laughs. 'It's a great smell, isn't it?'

Uncle Evan goes inside, but not before warning me again to 'stay out of the way' and Sondra and I walk back to the dairy shed and through the milking room and out to Rocket-Beau's yard.

When we get to the holding yard, Sondra introduces me to Chelsea. It turns out that Chelsea is actually her niece, not her daughter, and Sondra is here to give Chelsea a riding lesson.

'Hello,' Chelsea says, giving me a once over as she takes the bridle out of my hands.

From up close, I can see that Chelsea is extremely pretty. She looks like she might be in about Year 9 or even Year 10. She's quite small and petite in her navy blue jodhpurs and shiny black riding boots. She has straight blonde hair, big green eyes that are framed with mascara and a cute, turned-up nose. She wears simple little earrings that jiggle when she moves her head. I'm conscious of the fact that I'm a good deal younger than her but I'm probably taller. I hate being tall. I hate having wavy hair. I hate having freckles on my nose. I hate my faded blue jeans and cheap black gum boots.

'He's so beautiful,' I tell her, gesturing towards Rocket-Beau.

She gives a tight little smile but she doesn't answer. I watch as she sidles up next to her horse, gently slipping the bridle over his muzzle and up over his ears, her hands expertly placing the bit on his tongue. Sondra has placed the saddle on the rail of the holding yard, and I look on as Chelsea places the saddle mat on Rocket-Beau's withers, then tosses the saddle over his back. She squats down to fetch the saddle girth from beneath Rocket-Beau's belly and buckles it up, gently nudging Rocket-Beau in the ribs with her knee to make him breathe in. She places two fingers beneath the girth to make sure it's not too tight, then she slips on her navy blue riding hat, her neat ponytail sitting at the nape of her neck.

Before Chelsea mounts her horse, she opens the gate and takes him into the round yard and I stand outside the railing and watch as she lunges him with a long lead and a long whip. He strides out with his head tucked gracefully and his tail held aloft as she makes him trot and canter in both directions. It doesn't take long before I can see white sweat foaming on either side of Rocket-Beau's girth and between his front legs. After that, Chelsea unclips the long lunging lead and gathers the reins up in her hands. She stands up straight, facing the horse's rear end as she places her foot in the stirrup and then hoists herself up into the saddle.

Unbearable jealousy stabs me. I would give anything to be Chelsea, sitting atop this magnificent animal. My eyes tear up and threaten to spill over so that I have to look away. And then I turn back and look on as Chelsea canters around in circles with Sondra reminding her to keep her heels down, squeeze with her knees, keep her hands low.

When her lesson is finished, Chelsea brings Rocket-Beau back into the dairy shed. When she takes his saddle and bridle off, she hoses him down, then uses a rubber squeegee to scoop off the excess water. Sondra goes into the feed shed to mix up a bucket of feed for him, and Chelsea takes a comb to his mane and tail while he hungrily devours his oats and chaff, chomping and snorting. She's so confident around him that she stands directly behind his back legs, unafraid of being kicked.

Eventually, Rocket-Beau has finished his meal and Chelsea and Sondra have packed up and returned to their car. All the while, Chelsea hasn't spoken, but Sondra politely says goodbye and invites me to watch Chelsea ride Rocket-Beau tomorrow. I tell her 'thank you' and 'maybe' but as I watch the horse's owner disappear down the drive, I'm not sure that I could go through that again.

4

After lunch, Dad announces that we're going to the canal. June and I are instructed to change into our swimmers. Dad, Cameron and Mitchell set about putting lures on fishing rods. Mum chops watermelon in the kitchen and packs snacks and cold drinks in the esky. We all pile into the Valiant. Dad sits behind the steering wheel, his big, rough hands at ten and two. Mum rides in the front passenger seat, wearing her huge pair of sunglasses that she says, 'give her the air of a movie star'. We kids are crammed in the back, riding in the same places as always, Mitchell's bare sweaty thigh against mine. We're all holding our towels, and I try to tuck mine in between us so that I'm not touching him. I'm worried that this might make him angry or offended, but when I sneak a glance at his face, I can see he's amused.

We get to the canal, spilling out of the car in a jumble of arms and legs. June makes the mistake of getting out of the car without her thongs on and starts shrieking when her feet sting against the hot tar. Dad holds her in the air while I rummage around on the car floor, fishing her thongs out from underneath the driver's seat.

The canal is an inlet of shallow water. At this time of day, the tide is in and fishing should be good. Dad announces that he's going to catch enough fish to feed the family dinner. He tells us flathead is on the menu.

Mum isn't interested in fishing. We set up camp in the sand and she stays put, smearing half a bottle of reef oil on her long legs and lying outstretched on her beach towel immersed in one of her Mills and Boon novels.

June and I swim. There are no rough waves here at the canal, and even when the tide is in like this the water is clear and shallow. June and I can wade out really far and still stand up with our heads and shoulders above the water. I love swimming in the canal. I love swimming in the surf too, but it's hard to play games when the waves are crashing and the surf is rough. Here in the canal, the water is calm. June and I practise doing handstands. We do forward somersaults and backward somersaults, pinching our noses to avoid getting salty water up our nostrils. We play a game where we go under water and try to speak to one another, then come up to the surface and see if we can guess what the other is saying. We never have a clue, but it's a fun game.

After a long while, we come into the shore. We go get our buckets and shovels and set about building sandcastles. We dig a moat and carry water in our buckets to fill it and stack clumps of wet sand next to each other, making a big square.

'It looks a bit boring,' I tell June. 'We need to decorate it.'

But there are no shells on the sand here in the canal. There's no seaweed. The sand is clear and smooth, right up to the lip of the water. To our right, a long way along the shore, waves start to break, and we can see a few swimmers in the water.

'Let's take a walk to the surf beach,' I say. 'There'll be shells and seaweed there.'

I consider telling Mum. I look back to see she's facing away from us, buried under a wide-brimmed hat, deep in her book. I decide against it. We won't be long.

We walk along the shoreline, turning backwards to see our footprints in the sand. I find a stick and write our names. June wants the stick, and she draws a picture of a flower and a sun and makes little 'm' shapes for birds, flying in the sky.

We come across some shells. Some are smooth and grey. Others are orange and white, rough and corrugated. June holds one against her ear, trying to hear the ocean, but the shells are too small. There's seaweed too, and I add some to my bucket. I see some little holes in the sand. Dad has told me that if you dig deep enough, you might find a crab at the bottom of the hole. I settle down in the sand and start digging, using my shovel and tossing clumps of sand over my shoulder. And then a shadow falls across me.

'You didn't touch that, did you?'

I look up to see a woman's face silhouetted in the afternoon sun.

'They're poisonous. It'll sting you if you touch it,' she warns me. And with that, she disappears down the beach.

I look down and notice the blue-tailed bubble that is on the sand near my knee. I study my hand, bringing the fingertips close to my face.

Had I touched it?

There, on the pointer. I see a dot. I'm sure. And now, perhaps blood, seeping through to the surface of the skin. It starts to burn. I'm certain now. A heat is spreading through my hand and riding up my forearm.

I look back up the beach. I can only just make out my mother, her bright yellow costume a tiny blob in the distance. It's a long walk back. I look towards the other end of the beach. A few bodies are bobbing in the water. I watch one ride the white foam of a wave, clutching his boogie board, tilting his head to drain the water from his ear. There's a man there. Older. Maybe he's the surfer's dad. Should I go to him? Should I run into the surf and tell him I've been stung by a bluebottle? Will he hold me and tell me everything is OK? Suddenly, desperately, I want a grown up to tell me everything is going to be OK.

A volcano of panic erupts. At once the bluebottle's deadly venom is in my chest. I look at June. I need to speak. I need to hear my voice, to ground me, to bring me out of the terror inside my head. I say her name. 'June.' Again. 'June.' I can barely hear my own voice over the roar in my ears. June smiles at me, squatting, making long grooves in the sand with her fingertips.

A cricket bat connects with my ribcage. The pain is pulsing in time with my blood, pumping Bluebottle poison through my veins and filling my heart. It takes such an effort to stay upright that I lie back on the wet sand, relishing the cool against my skin.

My face is throbbing. My ears are burning. My heart is racing, my breathing rapid. Shallow. I wait for my heart to burst like a water balloon, foamy suds of the blue blob's venom coursing along my arms and legs.

I suppose I will faint, and I close my eyes and wait for the impending darkness.

But I don't faint. My heart doesn't explode. My breathing slows and the burning in my arm cools to a tingle. I look at June, squatting in the sand, oblivious to my terrifying brush with death. I try to stand. My legs feel weak, a strange fatigue washes over my whole body.

'Come on, June,' I say. 'Let's head back.'

*

When we get back, Mum has been so absorbed in her book that she hasn't even noticed we've been gone. I wonder whether she can see any lingering signs of terror on my face, but she simply sits up, brushes the sand off her thighs and says, 'Let's go see how the boys are getting on.'

Mum places a bookmark in her book, picks up her camera and loops it over her head. We wander down to the water. I feel a powerful urge to grab my mother's hand, but June is there first, slipping her outstretched fingers into Mum's fist. We walk down the sand bank and we all wade out to where the boys are fishing, knee deep in water. We discover Dad and the boys haven't caught any fish.

'Can I have a go, Dad?' June asks.

Dad puts some bait on the end of a rod and casts it out for her. Mum notices that June's shoulders are turning pink and Dad gives June his Hawaiian shirt, which billows on her like a bed sheet, her skinny legs sticking out the bottom.

Mum takes the lens cover off her camera. She wants a photo of June. She tells June to put on her oversized sunglasses and Mum and Dad laugh, but not in a bad way. They laugh as though they're delighted by the sight of June, her bob-cut, jet-black hair, the big sunglasses and brightly coloured shirt, the fishing rod in her hand. I can see how cute she looks and I feel like I might hate June right now.

After Mum takes a few snaps of June, I ask her to take a photo of me.

I stand in the water and bring one leg in front of the other. I place my hands on my hips and sort of pucker up my lips, not really smiling, the way I've seen the models do it in *Dolly* magazine.

Mum and Dad share a funny look and Mum wears a sort of laughing smile but she takes the photo and she says, 'You look very nice, Bridie. That will make a great photo.'

Cameron and Mitchell wade across the canal towards us. They announce that they've had enough fishing and want to go for a swim in the surf. June wants to investigate the rock pools and Mum says she will take her.

'Do you want to come, Bridie?' June asks.

I shake my head. 'I want to stay here and fish with Dad,' I tell her.

Mum and June move off and Dad sends me back to shore to get a hand reel. I wade back out to him and ask him to cast it out for me. He seems annoyed. He always gets annoyed when the fish aren't biting.

'How about you have a go at casting,' he says.

'What about bait?' I ask.

Dad digs into his pocket and brings out a little lure, bright green with black spots, and he attaches the lure to the end of my hand reel. Then he gives me the hand reel and tells me to unwind it a little, swing the end in a loop a few times and throw it out as far as I can. I follow his instructions. My lure plops into the water, not far in front of me. I can see it wiggling around underneath the surface of the water and the fishing line goes slack. To try to tighten the tension on the fishing line, I walk backwards a few steps in the water.

We stand there like that for a while, Dad holding his rod and me holding the hand reel. Dad reels his rod in a couple of times, tries changing the lure, then casts it out again. I start to get bored, and I think that maybe I should have gone to the rock pools with Mum and June. But then there's a tug on my line.

'I can feel a bite,' I tell Dad.

Dad laughs. 'The only thing you're going to catch today is a gumboot,' he tells me.

But I do feel a bite. The hand reel is nearly getting pulled out of my hands and I lift it up and try to twist it around, trying to shorten the fishing line. The water is crystal clear and I can make out a shadow in the sand, cast by the fish that is squirming at the end of my line.

'Shit!' I hear Dad say, and he quickly hands me his fishing rod and snatches the reel out of my hands. He twists the reel around and around and in moments the fish breaks through the surface of the water and dangles there, bucking on the end of my line.

'A bloody flathead,' he mutters.

This is the first time I've ever caught a fish. I think that my fish will make Dad happy, but it doesn't.

He shakes his head and says again, 'A bloody flathead,' and he takes my fish up to the shore where he can wrench it off the hook.

The hook is protruding through the mouth of the fish and I don't like to look at it, but I'm excited. I can't wait to see the faces on Cameron and Mitchell when Dad tells them I caught a fish. Maybe Mum will take a photo of me, proudly holding my fish like one of the photos of Dad on our fridge door.

Dad drops the fish in the bucket.

'Is it a good fish, Dad?' I ask him. 'Can you eat it?'

'You can,' he says.

I want to have another go. Now I want to fish all afternoon, dragging flathead after flathead out of the water. Dad and I leave my fish in the bucket on the shore and wade out again to our fishing spot. He casts his rod and I cast my hand reel. We stay there for what seems like ages, but no one gets another fish.

Eventually, Dad says it's 'quitting time' and we go into shore and back to our camp on the sand. Mum and June are there. When Mum sees us coming, she stands up and starts packing up, shaking sand off her towel and tucking her book into the big beach bag.

'Guess what?' I say when we're close enough.

'You caught a fish,' says Mum.

I nod a yes and look at Dad, hoping he might look proud. But he just tuts and shakes his head. 'She caught a bloody flathead,' he grumbles.

Mum laughs. Then she tells me to walk down to the surf and tell Cameron and Mitchell that we're leaving and that they need to come in. I don't want to. I don't want to have to walk back up the beach with Mitchell, but when I ask if Dad can do it, I get a stern look that convinces me not to say anything more.

I walk along the beach. I try to find the footprints and the drawings June and I made when we walked this way earlier, but the tide has come in even more and they've long since washed away. The surf is calm, the waves small and breaking close to the shore. When I see the boys, I wave my hands over my head and yell for them to come in, and when I know that they've heard me, I don't wait. I turn around and race back up the beach.

When we get home, Dad gets my fish out of the esky. He carefully removes the head and the scales and he wraps it up in foil with a piece of lemon and he puts it in the oven. Everyone sits down at the dinner table and Aunty Ruby dishes up a roast chicken with roast potato and roast pumpkin and peas and thick, rich gravy and it looks and smells delicious but Dad tells me I'm not allowed to have any and that my dinner is the fish that I caught. I nibble at the fish but it tastes disgusting and I say that I don't want it and Dad says, 'Too bad,' and I start to cry. Mum and Aunty Ruby tell Dad to ease up and not to force me to eat the fish but Dad booms, 'She caught a fish, she's going to eat a fish!' and he sounds so loud and angry that everyone shuts up and eats in silence while I sit there trying to stifle my sobs and after everyone has left the table, Dad says I have to stay there until the fish is gone.

I don't eat the fish. I can't eat the fish. And later, when everybody is watching television in the lounge room Aunty Ruby gives me a cuddle and says, 'You don't have to eat the fish,' and she takes it outside and drops it in the cat bowl.

*

We're sent off to bed early, and after our afternoon at the canal, I'm in such a deep slumber that when the strobing light slices through the window, I'm not sure whether I'm awake or dreaming. Slowly, I open my eyes to see a beam of light coming through the window next to the bed and flooding the room. I know it's still night-time because the light illuminates the room so brightly I can see the bed reflected in the cupboard mirror and I can make out the patterns of the tiles near the fireplace.

I sit up, swing my legs over the edge of the bed and scamper over to the window. The light is so blinding my eyes squint against it and I need to duck my head beneath the bottom of the window frame. I listen, carefully, and I hear the low grunt of a car engine. And there, on top of the revving, I hear voices. Men's voices. Calling out. Laughing, maybe.

The light is moving now, in and out of the room, slicing around like a light sabre. It fills the room then disappears, then turns around and floods the room again.

It's the boys, Cameron and Mitchell, with Dad and Uncle Evan. They're spotlighting.

When the light disappears, I pop my head up and sneak a look out the window. I see Uncle Evan's ute. It's not so far away, perhaps halfway down the house paddock. There's a huge floodlight attached to the metal frame on the back of Uncle Evan's ute. And I can see the boys, my brother and his friend, standing on the tray of the ute, hanging on to the frame as it zigzags through the paddock.

Suddenly there's a loud yell. I can't make out the words but I know it's Uncle Evan's voice. He's stopped the ute and he's calling out to the boys on the back. I see Cameron bend down close to the cab. I guess he's trying to hear what Uncle Evan is saying. Then he stands up again, and I watch him lift a rifle from off his shoulder and balance it on the roof of the cab. I hear a bang. Then another. One more. Then there's yelling. Whooping. Then a long, loud laugh.

The ute fires up and drives about thirty metres. The cab opens up and my Dad gets out, walks around the front of the vehicle, bends down and picks something up, holding it high. The boys holler and in the bright of the headlights I see it's a rabbit. Or maybe a hare. Dad holds it aloft by its long ears, swinging its lifeless body from side to side.

Dad walks to the back of the ute and tosses the limp creature onto the tray. Then, after wiping his hand on the back of his pants, he stretches it out towards my brother, who bends down and shakes it. Then Dad gets back in the ute and it spins around and heads down the hill towards the highway.

I crawl back into bed. June is lying on her back, snoring softly, and I roll onto my side facing her. Uncle Evan's floodlight is still chopping in and out and I can see June's silhouette. I watch the rise and fall of her chest and hear the soft pop of her lips each time she breathes out. I close my eyes and try to get back to sleep, but there's a sick feeling in my guts. My throat hurts and my eyes are wet. I roll onto my back and tears roll down my temples and into my ears.

Eventually, the light disappears altogether and I can't hear the engine of the ute any more. The room is quiet and dark but there's a throb in my chest. In my ears. I roll my head from side to side but I can't shake the image of my Dad, laughing, swinging the dead rabbit and shaking my brother's hand. I lie there wondering how old it was, whether it was a doe or a buck, whether it had kittens and what will happen to them now.

I move a little closer to June and feel something underneath my elbow. It's June's snuggle pillow. I press the button on the back and watch the merry-go-round of horses light up the ceiling. They glow and fade and dance in a circle and I focus on the horses. I imagine they're all mine. I imagine each horse has its very own stable with its name above the door. There's Casper and Kansas and Smokey and Polly and I spend each day riding one of them over the hill and down to the ocean, their muscly legs powering through the sand, their manes and tails swishing in the wind.

And that's what I try to think about as I lie on my back, watching the glowing horses pulse on the ceiling. But when I finally fall asleep, I dream of a litter of kittens curled up in their den, waiting for their mother to come home.

5

I wake to the sound of moaning. It doesn't feel like morning yet. It's still dark outside the windows and the rest of the house is silent. It's June, lying next to me, tears wet on her cheeks and her hand held over her left ear.

'What's wrong?' I ask her. But she just moans louder.

I tiptoe across the hallway and enter the opposite bedroom. Mum and Dad's bedroom.

'Mum,' I whisper loudly.

She's a light sleeper and her face crinkles instantly as she peers at me through the darkness. 'What's the matter?'

'It's June. She's crying.'

Mum pushes back the covers and follows me back into our room and pulls on the light switch. Bright light floods the room to reveal June, now sitting up in bed, crying loudly and rocking back and forth, both hands over her ear.

'Oh, June,' says Mum.

Dad appears at the door. 'What's going on?'

'June has an earache,' Mum says. She tells Dad to go searching for Panadol and Dad takes off down the hall. 'Come on, June. You come into bed with us.'

'Can I come into your bed?' I plead.

'Don't be silly!' Mum snaps. 'Turn the light off and go back to sleep!'

Mum and June disappear and I go back to bed, but I can't get back to sleep. I can still hear June crying from the next room and the muffled murmurs of Mum and Dad trying to comfort her. I lie awake and try to think happy thoughts. I imagine sheep jumping over a barrel, one...two....three...four...but a weight sits heavy in the base of my belly as the memory plays in front of my eyes. Dad swinging the lifeless rabbit. Mitchell, pulling on my hand. I feel sick again, and my eyes sting and my throat hurts and I hate June so much for waking me up and for sleeping in the bed between Mum and Dad and for leaving me alone in this dark room. I try to think about something else, but my thoughts turn to Samantha and the stupid boy and Chelsea and Rocket-Beau and I want to get out of bed and go outside and sit in the arms of the fig tree but I know Mum will hear me and order me back to bed, so I roll over and wipe my teary eyes and runny nose on the pillowcase and eventually I fall asleep.

When I wake again, the day is bright. I visit the outhouse and then find Aunty Ruby in the kitchen.

'Hello, sleeping beauty,' she teases me.

I look at the clock and it's already past nine.

'Where is everyone?' I ask.

'Your dad and the boys left early to go fishing, and your mum's taken June into town to see the doctor.'

I've missed my chance to go fishing or to go into town. I've probably even missed milking with Uncle Evan.

'Oh,' is all I can manage.

'Don't worry, love,' says Aunty Ruby. 'I've got some good news. Guess who's coming to visit today.'

I wonder if she's about to tell me that Samantha has ditched the stupid boy who doesn't even know her name and that she's coming specially to see me. I look at her expectantly, but it's not Samantha.

'Debbie!'

My face lights up with surprised delight. Aunty Ruby is right. This is good news.

'Oh, cool,' I say.

'So you can meet your new cousin Alex!'

I go and get dressed, wash my face and brush my teeth, and fix myself some cereal for breakfast. After that, I wander over to the milking shed. The shed is empty and freshly hosed out and Uncle Evan is nowhere to be found. I suppose he's somewhere on the property, mending some fences or tinkering with the pump down near the dam. I walk through the shed and find Rocket-Beau in his yard.

Rocket-Beau's coat is wet and his flanks shimmer in the sun. Clearly, Chelsea has already been and gone. I figure I'm alone and I dare to wriggle through the rail and stand on the other side of the fence, inside Rocket-Beau's yard. His ears must be itchy from the morning's sweat because he tilts his head and rubs it hard against my arm, almost knocking me off balance.

I go into the shed and notice that Chelsea and Sondra have left Rocket-Beau's saddle, bridle and bag of grooming gear in the shed. I fish a soft brush out of the bag and I start brushing his mane, first the tuft of hair between his ears and then the mane that falls gracefully down the side of his neck. He stands there contentedly, occasionally swatting the flies off his flanks with his long tail. I brush along his withers and his belly. I gingerly rub the brush along his front legs and as close to his hoof as I dare. I move to his rump, and his back legs. I want to brush his tail the way Chelsea did, standing behind him. I inch nervously around his hind leg, keeping at such a distance that I can barely reach his tail. Suddenly, his back leg lifts off the ground and I squeal with terror, certain he's about to kick me. But Rocket-Beau just stamps his leg back down on the ground, his twitching muscles sending a swarm of flies floating off. But I've been scared off and don't have the nerve to stand at his rear again.

I place the brush back in the bag and eye the saddle. I take in the delicious leathery smells. I feel the seat of the saddle smooth beneath my hands. I lift it up. It's quite heavy and Rocket-Beau lifts his head at the sound of buckles scraping along the ground. I actually consider throwing the saddle over his wither. I imagine buckling the girth around his belly, placing my foot in the stirrup and pulling myself up onto the horse, just like I watched Chelsea do. But I'm not that brave.

Instead, I place the saddle on the top rail of Rocket-Beau's yard. I pretend that I'm saddling up my own horse, a magnificent dappled grey, just like the stunning showjumper I saw on the television one Sunday afternoon. His mane is braided into tight rosettes and a blue ribbon is threaded through his tail. I buckle up the girth. I take the bridle and I hang it on a post, imagining I'm slipping it over the horse's velvety ears, placing the bit in his mouth and gathering up the reins.

I place a foot on the bottom rail and lift myself up, crawling up two more rails before seating myself in the saddle. For the tiniest moment, I'm there on top of my very own horse, but then I'm off balance and the saddle slips swiftly to the left. I fall, hitting the dirt ground hard, the saddle crashing down on top of me. I cry out and Rocket-Beau throws his head up, pinning his ears back and trotting, frightened, to the other side of his yard.

Pain shoots through my left arm. I grip it hard with my right hand, willing the pain away, but when I lift my hand, I can see bright blood. My arm is grazed beneath my forearm from my elbow to the wrist. It throbs and I curl into a ball, clutching my arm and sobbing quietly. I'm afraid. I'm afraid that the arm is broken. I'm afraid of the graze and the bruising, because I'm not allowed near the horse and I have no idea how I'm going to explain this injury.

Eventually, I sit up. The throbbing has died down and I can move my fingers, swivel my wrist. Not broken, I decide. But the graze is burning and there's blood and dirt on my T-shirt. I need to get the saddle and bridle back in the shed. I need to get back to the house, where Aunty Ruby will inspect my arm, and I need to get my story straight.

I struggle, only able to use my right arm to lift the saddle up and place it back on the pommel in Rocket-Beau's shed. I walk back through the shed and the idea gradually emerges, like a figure in the fog. The fig tree. I will tell Aunty Ruby I fell out of the fig tree.

Just to be safe, I actually go to the fig tree. I attempt to climb it with my one good arm but I can't quite pull my weight onto the lowest-hanging limbs. I look back towards the house to make sure

Aunty Ruby isn't watching me through the kitchen window and I pick up some dirt and some leaves and I rub it into my graze. The pain takes my breath away. I rub some dirt and leaves on my shirt and my jeans. I concentrate hard enough to bring on a fresh bout of tears and, armed with my fabrication, I head off into the house to find Aunty Ruby.

Aunty Ruby is sitting at the dining room table, flicking through a newspaper.

'Aunty Ruby,' I call out through my tears.

'What happened?' she asks, getting up and coming towards me.

I tell her I fell out of the tree.

'Jesus, Bridie,' she scolds. 'Will you ever learn?' But it looks like she's bought my story. She takes me into the kitchen and she cleans my graze. She paints it with Betadine and she puts a huge gauze over it. Then she wraps my arm from elbow to wrist in a bandage.

It's still hurting badly and I wince each time she moves it but I have to admit I'm really enjoying this special attention. When she's finished, she even makes me a treat; a plate of ginger snap cookies and a drink of ginger ale, and she sets me in front of the television.

After a little while, Mum comes home with June. The doctor says she has an ear infection and she's been given antibiotics. When Mum sees my arm, she says the exact same thing as Aunty Ruby. 'Bloody hell, Bridie, will you ever learn?' But she lightly touches the top of my head.

Then a little while later, Aunty Ruby tells us that Debbie's car is coming up the driveway.

June and I race out to meet her. We haven't seen Debbie since last summer holidays, before she had baby Alex, and when she gets out of the driver's seat I'm shocked at the sight of her. She doesn't look anything like the cousin I saw a year ago. She's dressed in a pair of tracksuit pants and a peach-coloured T-shirt. She's a lot bigger than the last time I saw her. Her ordinarily slender frame is hidden beneath a layer of soft flab, her tracksuit pants stretched tight across the top of her thighs. I can see her slack tummy hanging out of the bottom of her T-shirt. Her hair is back to her natural colour, a mousy brown. She doesn't even have any make-up on. She moves slowly, bending awkwardly across the backseat to undo the complicated mess of straps and buckles around the baby's capsule.

June doesn't seem at all thrown by Debbie's stunning transformation. She races towards the car, wrapping herself around Debbie's legs before she even has a chance to lift the capsule out of the car. 'Debbie!' she cries.

I move towards Debbie too, telling June to get out of the way and give Debbie some room. Callum comes racing around from his side of the car and June squeals again, giving Callum a squishy hug, who folds into his cousin's embrace and abruptly starts telling her about the action figure he holds in his hand. Mum and Aunty Ruby appear, kissing Debbie and making a big fuss of Callum and then we're all hovering over the capsule, hypnotised by the sight of the new baby, Alex, snoozing soundly in the baby capsule, little bubbles of spittle on his lips, popping and hissing with each little breath, a pale blue bonnet on his tiny head.

After a time, we go inside and Aunty Ruby puts the kettle on. Debbie wants to know what happened to my arm and I blurt out my lie. It feels dirty on the tip of my tongue and I quickly change the subject.

'How long are you staying, Debbie?' I want to know.

Everybody turns to her expectantly.

'Um…I'm not sure. Maybe a couple of days?'

'Where's Lachlan?' June asks. Lachlan is Debbie's husband.

'He's working,' says Debbie.

'Over the Christmas holidays?' my mum asks, incredulous.

'He had Christmas and New Year off, but he's back now. The business is flat out,' sighs Debbie.

'Well, I guess that's good news,' Mum says.

Debbie nods but says nothing.

'Debbie, will you do my make-up? Please?' I whine.

June's ears perk up at this. 'Oh, me too, me too?'

Debbie lets out an enormous sigh that seems to stem from the bottom of her thick legs. 'Not today, girls,' she tells us. 'Maybe later.'

The urge to protest bubbles up inside me, but as I watch Debbie's face, she lifts her eyes towards my mum, a strange expression crumpling her features. Her chin trembles just a little and her eyes grow wet with tears that cling to the lashes that frame her tired eyes. Mum turns to me. She doesn't need to say anything. I want to stay here and find out what's wrong with Debbie, but I know that look on my mother's face. I collect my sister and my cousin and we head outside.

We spend the entire afternoon playing. We play round after round of hide-and-seek.

Callum is talking a lot more than I remember. When he's in, he places his hands over his eyes and counts out loud; 'One…two…three…four…six…ten!'

It's too cute and June and I laugh our heads off. We play chasings around the house, jumping up onto the veranda, and when Callum is in, June and I slow down so that he can actually catch us.

I find some books in the spare room and we go out on to the veranda and I sit Callum and June on the steps and I pretend I'm the teacher and June and Callum are students in my class and I read them a couple of stories and I hold the book up so that they can see the pictures and I put on funny voices when the characters are talking.

After what seems like hours, Mum comes out to tell us the boys are back from fishing and we need to come inside and have a bath before dinner.

June and Callum and I all pile into the bathtub. I love the bathtub at Aunty Ruby's. At home, we usually have showers. We do have a bathtub but in comparison to Aunty Ruby's, it's a sink. At Aunty Ruby's, there's no shower, just the huge tub that has four big claws and is so long and deep that June and Callum and I can all fit in it together, squirming around and changing places, dunking our heads beneath the water and blowing huge clouds of bubbles in each other's faces. We laugh and squeal so much that Mum has to come in twice to tell us to 'keep the bloody noise down', warning me not to get the bandage on my arm wet.

June and Callum and I get dressed in our pyjamas and while Callum and June sit on the lounge room floor playing with Callum's blocks, I help Aunty Ruby set the table, as best as I can with my good arm. There are ten of us all together: Mum, Dad, Cameron and Mitchell, Aunty Ruby, Uncle Evan, Debbie, Callum, June and me. Aunty Ruby gives me a big jug of gravy, some mint sauce and the salt and pepper shakers to place in the middle of the dining room table. She opens up the oven door, the tantalising smells of roast lamb and garlic flooding the kitchen.

She calls out to Uncle Evan, asking him to come and carve the meat and she sings out to everyone else, 'Come on, everyone! Dinner is served!'

When I come out to the dining room table, there are only a couple of seats left. I pull out a chair at the head of the table and sit down next to Debbie, grabbing a bread roll from the basket and reaching for the butter.

'Bridie, that's Uncle Evan's seat. You know that. Come and sit here.' That's Mum, patting the seat next to her.

But on the other side of that vacant seat is Mitchell, looking at me now with a funny smirk on his face.

'Oh, why can't I sit here?' I begin, but of course, it's no use. My mother has spoken and I need to move.

That sick feeling washes over me as I slide into the seat next to Mitchell, careful not to let my bare leg rub up against him. But after a moment, Mitchell places his hand on my thigh, underneath the table. No one can see his hand. The tablecloth is hanging over the edge of the table, covering my leg and his hand. I want to push his hand away, but I'm afraid to say anything. I'm afraid he might get angry. I'm afraid he will act all innocent and call me a liar in front of everyone. I pull my leg away from him and pour myself a drink of water from the jug sitting in the middle of the table, gulping noisily as I throw it back.

Before we begin eating, Uncle Evan says, 'Who's going to say grace?'

Everyone goes quiet for a minute. I look at June and Cameron, Mum and Dad. Uncle Evan has never asked anyone to say grace before.

'Two – four – six – eight – dig in, don't wait!'

We all laugh and then everybody starts talking at once. Uncle Evan addresses us kids first, asking for our plates and loading them up with delicious meat, then passing the plate on to Dad, who serves up roast potato and pumpkin and peas and asks if we want gravy. It all looks, and smells, amazing, but I'm not really hungry. Sitting here next to Mitchell, I've lost my appetite. My arm is throbbing from my 'fall' from the fig tree and I feel hot tears stinging my eyes. I know I'll get in trouble if I don't eat, so I stuff the meat in my mouth and chew.

After dinner, Aunty Debbie and I collect all the plates and take them to the kitchen. Aunty Ruby brings out dessert: a cheesecake that Mum and Aunty Ruby made that afternoon, a jug of fresh cream and a big tub of ice cream. Aunty Ruby slices up the cake, placing each piece in a bowl and passing them around. But once again, I'm not very hungry.

'What's wrong with you? Are you feeling sick?' my mum jokes. 'It's not like you to not want to touch my cheesecake.'

'I'm just not very hungry,' I reply. And a strange quiet settles over the table for a moment. Mum is looking at me with squinty eyes and a furrowed brow and then Aunty Ruby and Debbie look at me too. I'm uncomfortable with the silence. And the looks. I pick my spoon up and shovel a mouthful of cheesecake into my mouth.

When the dinner and dessert is all cleared up, Mum, Dad, Uncle Evan, Aunty Ruby, Cameron and Mitchell sit around the dining room table. Dad and Uncle Evan drink beer and Mum and Aunty Ruby drink a peach-coloured drink from a big flask. They all play cards. They play a game called euchre and it always seems like a lot of fun. There's a lot of calling out and laughing. But I don't know how to play euchre and I don't want to stay at the table with Mitchell.

Instead, June and Callum and I start another game of hide-and-seek. We play round after round, hiding behind the Christmas tree, under the high double beds and behind the bathroom door. One time when June is in and I have to hide, I race into the spare room next to the bathroom where Debbie is staying. I want to hide in the tall cupboard. I open the door and climb up, shutting the door behind me. The cupboard is empty save for a couple of blankets folded up at the bottom of it and there's plenty of room. I hear June sing out, 'Ready or not, here I come,' and not long after that, I hear the bedroom door open. I figure June has found me already and I peek out through the cupboard door. But it isn't June at all. It's Debbie.

Debbie enters the room and shuts the door behind her. She has baby Alex in her arms and I can hear him whimpering and giving out a sort of half-cry. Debbie sits on the bed and lifts up her shirt. She pulls at her bra and drops a little triangle of fabric, revealing her nipple, enormous and brown, in the middle of a white breast lined with dark green veins. I can't help thinking it reminds me of the dairy cows lining up for morning milking. I watch, fascinated, as Debbie cradles Alex near her breast, and his little mouth latches on to the nipple and his crying stops. I can hear him sucking and making gurgling, breathing noises, something like a cross between humming and grunting.

Then I hear another noise. The unmistakable sound of crying; huge, explosive sobs that shatter the air in the dark room. I look at Debbie's face, her features collapsing, fat tears spilling down her cheeks. She wipes them away with her free hand and she tries to hold her body still so the baby can feed but her whole body is shaking, her shoulders shuddering up and down with each new burst of sobs. I don't know what to do. I feel ashamed now, that I stayed hidden in the cupboard and didn't make myself known to her when she first entered the room. And now I can't come out, because I don't want Debbie to know I've witnessed what has just taken place.

I can hear the sound of footsteps running down the hallway outside the bedroom. I can hear Callum squealing and I'm certain they will come into the bedroom and find me any minute. But they don't. The footsteps disappear down the hallway and the room is quiet, except for the sounds of Debbie's crying, easing now, and her baby gurgling and slurping at her breast.

I stay in the cupboard and watch as Debbie moves Alex on to the other nipple and lets him feed. After what seems like forever, she moves Alex's mouth away from her breast, doing up the straps on her bra and bringing her shirt back down over her flabby tummy. She puts Alex up on her shoulder and rocks him, patting his back, softly and slowly. In the dim light I can just make out her face, staring out through the window and off into the distance. Eventually, she places Alex in the portable cot that Uncle Evan helped her assemble earlier, and she leaves the room, going through the second door and into the bathroom.

I open the cupboard door, careful to be quiet, and I leave the room through the other door.

*

Later, lying next to June in bed, she asks me, 'What happened to your arm, Bridie?'

'What do you mean?' I say. 'I already told you, I fell out of the fig tree.'

After a long moment, June replies, 'No, you didn't.' And she rolls over and falls asleep.

6

I'm up early, in time to help Uncle Evan with the milking. My arm is still a bit sore, and when I lift the bandage up to inspect the graze, I can see blue bruising coming out on my skin. I'm not much help with the milking, but it's nice to be in the shed with Uncle Evan, taking in the rich mix of smells and watching him bring each cow into the milking shed to chomp on bran while they're milked. I sit quietly on the bottom rail of the fence, patting Jess and Bell when Uncle Evan isn't looking.

When the last cow has been turned out and Uncle Evan has hosed down the shed floor, he asks me whether I'd like to see the horse. I nod an enthusiastic yes. Together, we walk around the corner to the other side of the shed, where Rocket-Beau stands to attention, his ears pointed forwards, his nostrils flared. I imagine he's sucking in the freshness of the ocean on the breeze.

'He's so beautiful,' I tell Uncle Evan.

'Yes, he certainly is a handsome horse,' Uncle Evan agrees. 'He'd wanna be, the bloody money they paid for him.'

Uncle Evan moves into Rocket-Beau's shed and returns with a handful of lucerne hay. He gives it to me so that I can feed Rocket-Beau, who must be hungry, because he comes trotting over, whinnying quietly.

'I wish he was my horse,' I sigh.

'I know you do,' Uncle Evan says.

And I wonder then, not for the first time, whether I could move to Uncle Evan and Aunty Ruby's farm. Maybe I could change schools and live here, and Mum and Dad and Cameron and June could visit me on holidays and then I could have my own horse and go riding any time I liked. Maybe Chelsea and I could even be friends, taking long trail rides together, cantering our beautiful horses over the hill and along the beach. My head runs away with the fantasy, a pleasant feeling of joy and excitement bubbling up inside of me and bursting against my insides.

'Maybe when you grow up,' Uncle Evan says, 'you can have your own horse. Maybe when you grow up, you'll marry a farmer, and you can have a dozen horses.'

His comments shoot me down. Being 'grown-up' feels like a long time away. A lifetime. And I don't much like the idea of marrying a farmer. I don't much like the idea of getting married at all. I'm not really sure what it involves, but for some reason I think about Mitchell and the bulge in his shorts and the sick feeling in the pit of my stomach fires up again.

Rocket-Beau eats the last of his hay and we head back to the house. We kick our boots off at the door and go inside to see that breakfast is happening at the dining room table. Mum, Aunty Ruby and Debbie are sipping coffee and eating toast. June and Callum sit at the other end of the table, spooning Fruit Loops into their mouths. I take a seat and help myself to some orange juice and a piece of toast. Uncle Evan goes into the kitchen and returns to the table with a coffee and settles in at the head of the table, the newspaper spread out in front of him.

I ask Mum what we're going to do today.

'Not a lot,' she replies. 'Relax.'

That is the worst answer. When grown-ups say something is 'relaxing', you can bet it's boring. I tell her this and get a stern look from Mum and Aunty Ruby, warning me not to be so cheeky.

'Can we please go to the beach?' I ask.

June looks up, alert now. She knows this conversation is just as much about her as it is about me.

'No way,' answers Mum. 'I've had enough sun over the last few days.'

My face drops and my shoulders sag.

'I'll take you to the beach, Bridie,' says Debbie.

'Yes!' both June and I yell out, punching our fists in the air.

'Yes!' Callum copies us, punching the air and smiling up at his mother.

'Hang on a minute,' Mum interjects with an ominous tone. 'Bridie, you can go to the beach, but June, you're not going anywhere near the water with an ear infection.'

'Oooohhhh,' June complains, loudly. Her eyes fill with tears that spill out and trickle over her quivering bottom lip. 'That's not fair! Bridie's got a sore arm. Why is she allowed to go to the beach?'

I panic momentarily, but Mum says the salt water might actually be good for my grazed arm. June continues to protest, but I don't stick around to watch the struggle between my mum and June. I'm skipping up the hall, getting changed into my swimming costume. I know better than to say it, but I'm glad June isn't allowed to go to the beach. I'm glad that it will just be me and Debbie.

It takes a long time to get ready to go to the beach. Debbie says we're taking Callum, but she's leaving baby Alex at home with Aunty Ruby. This means she has to 'express' because Alex will need a feed while we're gone. Debbie disappears into the spare bedroom and after what seems like ages, returns to the kitchen with a small amount of milk in a small bottle that she places in the fridge.

Debbie's car is parked out by the fig tree. We put Callum in his booster seat and with a final warning from Mum about behaving myself, I get in the front seat. As Debbie reverses the car and points it towards the end of the driveway, I can see June's face crumple beneath a new batch of tears. I work hard to stifle a grin.

On the way to the beach, Debbie talks more than I've heard her talk since she arrived. She seems, if not happy, at least not as distraught as the Debbie I had witnessed from my hiding place in the cupboard. She asks me about school. I tell her it's OK. She asks me whether I've seen Samantha since I arrived. I tell her I haven't. She asks me whether I have a boyfriend. I tell her as if!

Debbie laughs. 'Surely you've got a crush on somebody,' she teases. 'Someone at school maybe?'

I shake my head vigorously. 'Nope,' I say.

'You won't be saying that for much longer. I'll bet you have a boyfriend the next time I see you.'

And then there's that sick feeling in my tummy, a darkness washing over me in an instant. It almost has a sound, like the walloping whip of a sheet of tin. I'm thinking about Mitchell and my hand tingles and tears sting at my eyes. And I can't hold them back, hard as I try. I start crying right there in the front seat of Debbie's car.

'Hey, hey,' she says soothingly. She reaches across to pat my thigh and I flinch at her touch. 'I'm sorry, Bridie. I didn't mean to upset you.'

I wipe at my eyes with the back of my hand. I wind the window all the way down so that the hot air blasts against my wet face.

'What is it, Bridie?' asks Debbie. 'Is something the matter? You can tell me.'

And I think about telling her. I think that I want to tell her. I know that I can't tell Mum or Aunty Ruby or June, but maybe I could tell Debbie. But I can't make the words come out of my mouth. I can't even make the words take shape in my head. I just shake my head and say, 'I'm fine. It's nothing. I'm fine.'

Debbie's not convinced. Her face still looks confused and concerned, but she keeps her eyes on the road and drops the questions.

I stare out the window, taking in the rolling green paddocks, the cows and the horses and the houses and the passing cars. A train rattles along the track, overtaking Debbie's little car and heading off into the distance as we turn off at the beach road. Soon, the road is lined with palm trees and I see the ocean, sparkling like a bed of diamonds in the south coast sunshine. I lick my lips and taste the ocean on my tongue.

Debbie finds a parking spot right near the little laneway that cuts through the grassy dunes and brings us out between the flags. We spread our towels out on the sand and Debbie helps me unwrap the bandage on my arm.

'Ouch, that looks nasty,' she says, tutting at the yellow scab that's forming near the elbow.

I agree, it feels a little nasty, although to be honest, it's much better than it was yesterday.

We head down to the water. Despite the heat of the day, the water is cool, and I wade in slowly, tucking my hands up under my chin as each wave crashes against my goose pimpled legs. When I'm in halfway up my torso, the water takes my breath away. I look back at Debbie, standing on the shoreline, hands on her wide hips, while Callum runs back and forth on the hard, wet sand, playing tag with the dancing shoreline.

In one swift move, I throw myself beneath a wave, fully immersing myself in the ocean. I can see and hear and feel the tumult of the wave above my head, and I let my arms swim out beside me, throwing my head back and slowly floating up to the surface. I wade out further, beyond the breaking waves to where the sea is calmer, and I bob up and down, letting each watery crescendo lift my feet up off the ocean floor and bring me closer to the sky.

I stay in the water a long time, but eventually I start shivering and I make my way back to shore. Debbie is sitting on her towel, not too far from Callum, who is digging with a little shovel in the wet sand. I towel myself off and join Callum, helping him make a long tunnel in the sand. I show him how to fill his little bucket with water and bring it to the top of the deep groove, pouring the water in and watching it run back out into the ocean. I laugh each time he tries to block the flow of water off with his tiny hands, convinced he has a chance to stop it with each new attempt.

Suddenly, I wonder what June is doing. I picture her distraught face as we drove away from the house. I wonder how long she kept up the crying after we'd gone. I imagine Mum is reading a book and Aunty Ruby is doing some sewing and Dad and the boys are out fishing and I suppose June is all alone. I picture her sitting on the veranda, kicking her legs back and forth, staring down the driveway and waiting for Debbie's car to appear at the gate. I feel a pang of guilt. I should have asked Mum to let June come to the beach. She could have stayed on the shore. She could have swum without getting her head wet, without getting water in her ear. I decide that when we get home, I'll play a game with June. We'll play teachers, and instead of making June be a student in the class like I always do, I'll let June be the teacher. I'm comforted by the thought of how happy it will make her.

When the sun is low in the sky, Debbie stands up, casting a long shadow in the sand. She brushes sand off her heavy thighs and shakes the sand out of her beach towel. 'I guess we should be getting home,' she announces.

I nod in agreement. My belly is rumbling with hunger and I realise lunchtime has long been and gone, but I haven't had anything to eat since breakfast. I pick up my towel and shake the sand out, throwing it over my shoulder so that I can help carry Callum's bucket and shovel. Debbie picks up her bag and tells Callum that he has to carry his own little sandals. We all head up the laneway and back towards the car.

At the car, Debbie throws her bag in the boot and looks down at the sandals Callum has dropped on the ground. They're covered in thick, wet sand. 'Oh, Callum,' she groans. 'Take those sandals down to the water and rinse them off. When you bring them back, I don't want to see any sand on them. Off you go.'

Callum trots off down the laneway with a sandal in each hand. Debbie gives everything another good shake, flicking the towels, slapping her thongs together and brushing at her feet. Sheets of fine sand rain down onto the tar. She shuts the boot and moves towards the front of the car, placing the keys in the ignition.

'I'm starving,' I tell Debbie.

'Me too,' she says. 'How about I buy us some hot chips at the milk bar on the way home?'

'Yum,' I say, smiling.

'Bridie,' she says. 'Can you go keep an eye on Callum?'

I walk down the laneway, coming out at the top of the sand dune. The beach is virtually deserted. There are no swimmers in the ocean and the flags have been taken down. I can see a couple of surfers, way out beyond the waves, paddling on the flat surface of the sea. When I look to my right, I can make out a couple walking hand in hand, their tall, sleek dog running out ahead of them. But I don't see Callum.

I walk all the way down to the water. I scan the surf. I look up and down the beach, as far as I can see in both directions. But I don't see Callum.

In the water, something catches my eye. A flash of red, rolling in the ocean foam. I move towards it, bend down to pick it up.

It's Callum's sandal.

I run back up the sand dune, through the laneway, yelling out to Debbie before I even reach the car.

'Debbie! Debbie!'

Debbie turns. Alarmed. She can hear the urgency in my voice. She moves towards me. I lift up the lone sandal, hooked on the end of my finger. Debbie races past me, heading for the ocean. I follow, uselessly. We reach the water, standing there together now, staring out to where the sea line meets the sky, staring out at all the emptiness in between.

Callum is nowhere.

Debbie turns to me. 'Where did he go?'

'I…I don't know,' I stammer.

'What do you mean, you don't know? I asked you to keep an eye on him!'

I've never heard Debbie sound so angry and my eyes well up, threatening to spill over.

Debbie spins in circles, squinting her eyes, scanning the sand and the grassy dunes beyond them, staring down the beach, curved like a slice of melon, all the way to the rocky cliffs at the other end. She turns her head the other way, towards the rock pools. A lone fisherman stands on the edge of a cliff, waves crashing against the rock face, splashing white water across his feet.

And still, there's no Callum.

Debbie starts yelling. 'Callum! Callum!' She throws her whole body into it, leaning forward and pushing out the long vowels. 'Caaaaalluuuum!' She calls to the ocean. She calls to the beach. She calls to the grassy dunes and the rock pools.

She walks up the beach, a long way, me lagging behind, not sure what I'm supposed to be doing. She turns around, walks back to the spot where she sent Callum to go wash the sand off his sandals. But Callum is nowhere.

A strange sensation takes over me now. The hunger I felt only minutes ago has disappeared. I feel a familiar sick in my tummy, and the flesh on my arms is tingling, the hairs lifting up off my skin. I look at Debbie's face. Her eyes seem focused elsewhere now. She's no longer surveying the scene. Instead, it seems her eyes look inwards, and I imagine the pictures taking shape in her mind. I imagine she sees a police car, blue lights flashing in the dusk. I imagine she hears the crackle of a two-way radio. She sees a tracker dog, lunging and tugging at its taut leash, nose to the ground. And then, I suppose, she sees her little boy. Perhaps he's hurt. Maybe he's bleeding. Maybe he's not breathing. Maybe he's floating, face down in the ocean. Maybe he's in the back of someone's car. Maybe…

Debbie shakes her head, trying to loosen the images, trying to throw the pictures off the screen. I stand beside her, my thumb between my teeth. The sun is getting lower and the cool breeze off the water makes my skin prickle. Debbie tells me she's heading back down the beach again. She instructs me to go the other way, towards the fisherman on the cliff, to search in the rock pools. She leaves and I move off in the opposite direction.

I get to the rock pool. I climb up on the boulder and I jump from rock to rock, looking in each pool as though I might find Callum there, amongst the shells and seaweed and broken glass. I go out as far as I can, eventually standing on the same rock surface as the fisherman. He turns to me. Smiles and nods. I suppose that I should ask him if he's seen a little boy. But I'm too shy. I don't know this man and I'm too afraid to open my mouth. And I can't imagine Callum made it up this far. His little legs couldn't jump the distance between the boulders. I turn and start descending the rock pools.

When I launch off the final boulder and I'm back on the sand, I notice a little opening at the side of the boulder. I poke my head inside and follow it around, to where it leads underneath the boulder into a small, dim cave.

And there is Callum.

He's squatting on the sand, like a little girl peeing, and when he sees me he squeals with laughter, 'You found me!'

7

How Callum reached the end of the beach to hide in the rock pools so quickly remains a mystery, as does the whereabouts of his second sandal. After hugging the life out of him, Debbie goes off her brain, warning Callum to 'never, never run away and hide like that again'.

We pick up hot chips on the way home, the tantalising smell of the salt and vinegar torturing my rumbling stomach in the car.

When we get home, Debbie tears open the parcel of hot chips and places them in the middle of the dining room table. She gets plates and tomato sauce from the kitchen and invites everyone to help themselves. As we tuck into the hot chips, Debbie tells Aunty Ruby and Mum about Callum's disappearing act.

While we're all eating, Dad, Uncle Evan and the boys burst through the back door. They've had a good day fishing and Dad and Uncle Evan set about preparing and cooking the fish in the kitchen. They've also bought a big bag of prawns, and soon they're on a big platter in the middle of the dining room table. Mum, Dad, Aunty Ruby, Uncle Evan and Debbie, even Cameron and Mitchell, rave about the prawns, popping their heads off, flicking the shells off their backs, squeezing a few drops of lemon on them and wolfing them down. Dad offers to peel me a prawn, but like always, I refuse. I hate prawns.

'June, you'll have a prawn, won't you?' says Dad. Dad peels a prawn for June, soaks it in lemon juice and gives it to her, watching her proudly as she chews and swallows enthusiastically. 'See?' Dad says, looking at me. 'Your sister's no fool.'

By the time we finish our seafood feast, the sun is setting and Cameron suggests a game of Murder in the Dark. I'm surprised that

Cameron has invited June and me to play a game with him and Mitchell, but I suppose that Murder in the Dark is more fun with more people. Cameron finds a torch and tells me I'm the first one to be 'in'.

I take the torch and Cameron tells me I'm to stand in the laundry, keep my eyes closed and count slowly to twenty. I move into the laundry while Cameron, Mitchell and June take off in all directions.

After counting to twenty, I turn the torch on, go through the laundry door and head outside. I shine the torch out into the dark, searching for any sign of Cameron, Mitchell or June. There are few stars in the night sky and the torch beam slices through the dark. I swirl it in circles and I find Cameron first. He's halfway up the fig tree, straddling one of its limbs like a sleeping koala.

'Got you!' I call.

Next, I move around the house and step up on the veranda. I creep along the wall, the torch beam lighting a path across the rickety floorboards. I round the corner and find June, pressed flat against the wall.

'Got you, June!' I yell, shining the torch on her.

I wander all the way around the house, but Mitchell is hard to find. I check the outhouse. I scan the paddocks. I go around the milking shed. Just when I think perhaps he's hidden inside the house, I find him squatting behind the rusty shell of a car in one of the dilapidated sheds on the other side of the fig tree.

Cameron is in next because he was 'murdered' first. We all run off to hide and are eventually found. June has a go at being in, then finally it's Mitchell's turn.

While Mitchell is counting, I make my way over to the milking shed. I quietly tug on the piece of rope that opens the door and slip inside, shutting the door behind me. I inhale deeply, relishing the smell of the cows, the bran, the hay, the delicious scent of Rocket-Beau. I move into the shed and slip inside one of the cattle crushes, squatting in a feed trough.

I listen for the sounds of the game outside. I listen for the voices of

Cameron and June and Mitchell, but it's eerily quiet and so dark I can barely make out my hand in front of my face. I hear the sound of my breathing and the thump of my heartbeat in my ears. And then I hear the slow creak of the milking shed door. The torchlight cuts a path through the shed, followed by Mitchell who shines the torch on me and whispers loudly, 'Murder!'

I step out of the cattle crush and move towards him. I try to get past him, to go through the door and out of the milking shed, but Mitchell puts a firm hand on my shoulder and stops me in my tracks.

'Hey,' he says. 'Where are you going?'

I don't understand the question. 'You found me,' I say.

'What's the rush?' he asks me, placing two hands on me now, one on each shoulder, and pressing down hard. My tummy flips and my body floods with the sickness. 'You don't like me much, do you, Bridie?' Mitchell says.

I don't know what to say. I've never even thought about whether I like him or not. All I know is I'm afraid of him. But I'm too afraid to tell him that.

'I like you,' I say.

'Do you?' A beat. 'So show me. Show me how much you like me.'

Mitchell takes my hand. He pulls it towards his crotch and I'm shocked to feel a hard lump there, underneath my hand.

'Have you ever kissed a boy, Bridie?' he asks.

I'm speechless, and shake my head, no.

He leans in, pressing his mouth on mine. I feel his tongue enter my mouth, poking around, hard and fast and wet. He keeps his hand on my hand, pushing it into his hard lump.

I'm limp. Still. My hand is floppy in his, my mouth is still, passive against his invasion. He pulls away. It feels like half my face is wet and I wipe at my mouth with the back of my free hand.

Mitchell keeps his face close to mine, looking me in the eyes. And then, he pulls back, drops my hand and takes a step back. 'Ah,' he says. 'You're frigid.'

I don't know what that means, but it doesn't sound good. It seems I've upset him, disappointed him. He turns around and leaves the shed. He doesn't ask me to follow him, so I stay there, still and silent in the quiet, dark shed. And then my body starts to tremble. My hands are shaking and my heart is pounding and my eyes brim with tears and I think perhaps I'm going to throw up.

I stay there a long time, just standing in the shed and waiting for the tears to go. I hear the noises outside of Cameron and June being 'murdered' in the dark, and I hear Mitchell saying that he hasn't found me, and then I hear all three of them come into the shed.

Mitchell shines a torch on me and says, 'Got you!'

Cameron says that June is in but I announce that I don't want to play any more. I go inside the house. Mum and Aunty Ruby and Debbie are sitting at the table. They're sipping tea and Debbie is nursing baby Alex in her arms. Callum is at the table too, propped up on a pillow, drawing.

'Hey, Bridie,' says Mum.

I feel all sick and cold and I ask Mum if I can have a bath.

Mum looks at me strangely. 'What's up?' she asks.

'Can I please have a bath?' I say again.

'Well…sure you can,' she says. 'Are you sure you're all right?'

I nod, but say nothing, and Mum gets up to run a bath for me.

When I'm in the bath, I bring my knees up to my chin and wrap my arms around my legs and the tears come anew. I cry so hard my head hurts, and it's an effort to keep my sobs under control, to keep the noise down so that Mum or Aunty Ruby or Debbie won't hear me and come into the bathroom and ask me what's wrong. I stay in the bath so long that the water goes cold and I have to top it up with hot water a few times before I get out.

With my pyjamas on, I go out into the dining room and sit next to Mum. I put my arms around her and rest my head on her shoulder. I want to feel her wrap her arms around me. I want to feel her kiss me on the top of the head. I want her to stroke my hair and let me sit in her lap, the way June does. I want her to say that she loves me. I want her to tell me I'm safe.

After a while, June comes inside. She tells us the boys have found another game that doesn't include her. She seems a little upset. I tell her to come and sit next to me. I put my arms around June and I tell her she doesn't need the boys. I tell her the boys' games are stupid and I tell her I'll always play with her. Mum, Aunty Ruby and Debbie all give me a long look and then I note the strange glances between them, but nobody says anything.

All of a sudden, there's a loud cracking sound from outside. It sounds like a gun going off, a rapid, stuttered rattle. It slices the quiet air in the dining room, and behind the noise is the high-pitched yelp of a dog. Mum and Aunty Ruby stand up and move towards the door. Uncle Evan and Dad come out from the lounge room, following Mum and Aunty Ruby.

'What the bloody hell was that?' yells Dad.

June and Debbie and I stay seated at the table but our ears are pealed.

In a moment, we hear Dad's baritone boom. 'What the bloody hell do you think you're doing?'

We hear Cameron and Mitchell mumble something in return, then more yelling from Dad. Eventually, Cameron and Mitchell come inside, walking shame-faced through the dining room and up the hallway towards their bedroom.

Dad orders them to stay there until he tells them they can come out again, 'which won't be for a bloody long time, I can tell you!' he adds.

'What did they do?' Mum asks.

Dad explains that the boys had bungers, rows of little firecrackers. They'd attached a line of bungers to the dog's tail and set them alight. Mum and Aunty Ruby and Debbie are horrified. Uncle Evan tells us the boys 'frightened the life' out of the dogs and he wouldn't be surprised if they'd both gone deaf.

The rest of the night, June and I enjoy our elevated rank as the children who didn't tie a row of firecrackers to the dog's tail and aren't in a world of trouble. We have ice cream with sprinkles for dessert and we're even allowed to eat it in the lounge room in front of the television, watching Loony Tunes cartoons. There's comfort in the colours and the music and the taste of the ice cream and the faces of the grown-ups asking us if we're OK each time they pass through the lounge room.

But the sickness in my tummy is still there, a flickering little pilot light that rears up each time I remember the milking shed, the pressure of Mitchell's hand on mine, his hard, wet tongue flicking around my mouth.

8

It rains overnight, and in the morning it's still drizzling lightly. Uncle Evan tells me to put on one of the Drizabones hanging from the coat rack in the hallway. It weighs a ton and the sleeves hang well over my hands. It smells like dirty boots but I wrap it around me, happy to be sitting behind Uncle Evan on the quad bike, bringing in the cattle. We drive around the paddock and when I get off the bike, there's mud splattered all over the back of me.

My arm is feeling better. It doesn't hurt so much, and I help Uncle Evan by filling the feed troughs with bran and lucerne hay. The cows munch lazily, lowering their long lashes beaded with raindrops over their huge, dark eyes.

When we're finishing up and Uncle Evan is hosing out the shed, Chelsea and Sondra arrive. Sondra says hello and she and Uncle Evan have a chat about the rain and the price of feed. Chelsea is wearing skin-tone jodhpurs and a T-shirt with the name of a band on it that I've never heard of. Her black boots are clean and shiny and her little earrings jiggle in her ears. I watch as she expertly takes Rocket-Beau's rug off, cleans out his hooves and saddles him up.

Today, Chelsea doesn't have a riding lesson. She doesn't lunge Rocket-Beau in both directions then ride him in circles. Instead, once he has his saddle and bridle on, Chelsea brings him through the round yard across to a second gate that opens out on to the big paddock where Uncle Evan's dairy cows graze. Chelsea mounts him, then turns towards the hill and digs her heels in.

I watch with such a pang of jealousy my fists ball up, as Rocket-Beau takes a few short strides then picks up to a full gallop, stretching his neck out long, his front legs almost floating. His mane

66

moves in the wind and his tail swishes out behind him, the muscles rippling in his powerful rump and hind legs.

Chelsea gallops Rocket-Beau all the way to the bottom of the hill. When she reaches the dam, she brings him back to a trot, making her way around the wide body of water and taking him up to the fence line that runs alongside the highway. She turns his head towards the driveway and I surmise that she's probably going to go down the driveway, take him through the gate and out onto the highway. I picture her trotting along the shoulder of the road, the cars passing by, each one admiring this pretty girl sitting on top of her stunning mount. I figure she's taking Rocket-Beau to the beach to canter along the shoreline, Rocket-Beau's hooves flicking sand and sea in his wake.

While Uncle Evan and Sondra keep talking, I head back inside the house. I don't want to think about Chelsea cantering along the beach on Rocket-Beau.

When I kick my boots off and hang the Drizabone up on the coat rack, I walk into the dining room. There's no one sitting at the table, but I can hear voices coming from the kitchen. Soft, low voices. I creep up the hall and stand just outside the kitchen door. One of the voices is Debbie, and she's trying to talk through tears, clearly upset.

'I can't do it, Mum,' she sobs, her voice high and thin.

And then Aunty Ruby speaks. 'Of course you can, Deb.'

'It's too hard, with Lachlan at work…'

'How do you think I felt, with you and Peter here and your dad down in the bloody paddock all day?'

I hear my mum, too. 'Debbie, you'll be OK. It's hard, but you'll be right.'

'But it wasn't like this last time,' cries Debbie.

I want to hear more. I strain to hear more, but no one speaks. I just hear Debbie crying and the sounds of a teacup being placed on a saucer and maybe the sound of Aunty Ruby stroking Debbie's arm.

I don't want to be caught eavesdropping at the kitchen door. I turn and quietly walk down the hall again, making a show of coming in through the back door this time, slamming it quite hard and coughing to announce my presence. I hear somebody, probably Debbie, sniffle and blow her nose, and my mum exits the kitchen and meets me in the dining room.

'Hey, Bridie,' she says, all bright and chirpy. 'You going to have some breakfast?'

I sit at the table and Mum brings me some hot toast and a Milo. I wonder aloud where Cameron and Mitchell are, and Mum informs me with a furious look that the boys are confined to their room today, still being punished over the incident with the firecrackers in the dog's tail.

After breakfast, I find June and Callum. They're out on the veranda playing a game. I can't even tell what the game is supposed to be about. They're just running around the house squealing, being babies. I ask them if they want to play a game with me. I try to stop June by standing in front of her as she runs around the corner, but instead of answering me she screams and pushes right past me, followed by Callum. I give up and go to the fig tree.

When I get there, I step up onto one of the tree's huge roots and pull myself up into one of the tree's low forks. I see the names of my brother and my cousins scratched into the tree. There's CAMERON in big, angular block letters. There's Debbie, with a little love heart for the dot above the 'I'. And a little way up the trunk is PETER. I've tried, a couple of times, to scratch my own name into the tree, but I don't seem to have the strength or skill to etch deep enough, and it always fades away. When I asked Cameron to do it for me once, he told me no, it was something I had to do for myself. I sigh and sink back into the trunk.

From my position up here in the tree, I can see all the way to Samantha's house. I wonder what she's doing. I wonder why she hasn't wandered up the dirt road over the past few days and come to visit me, knowing we're here. I wonder whether her and the stupid boy who doesn't know her name are doing schoolwork right now.

I look around, taking note of what else I can see. From here, I can see the roof of Uncle Evan and Aunty Ruby's house. I can see a frisbee on the roof, bright green and split, and a tennis ball stuck in one of the gutters. I can see all the way across the top of the milking shed, to the herd of cows slowly meandering away from the shed, down to the dam to drink and graze on the green grass.

In the other direction, I can see the bottom of Uncle Evan and Aunty Ruby's driveway, and the road on the other side of the gate that turns onto the highway that snakes over the hill. Soon, I'll be back on that road, squished in the back of the Valiant, Mitchell's sweaty thigh stuck up against mine.

I sit in the tree for a long time. Thinking. My thoughts go around in a loop, swirling like the fresh milk in the milking shed vat. I think about Mitchell, his hand, my hand, his crotch, his mouth, my mouth. And I think about that word. Frigid. I try to imagine what it means. It sounds like the word 'refrigerator' but that doesn't make any sense. Why would he say I'm a refrigerator?

Something moving in the distance catches my eye. It's Chelsea, trotting back along the fence line on Rocket-Beau. I watch as she walks him down the hill, leaning far back in the saddle as Rocket-Beau lowers his head and treads sure-footedly down the incline, swerving around small bushes and potholes. When she reaches the dam, Chelsea wades Rocket-Beau into the water, where he takes a long drink, thirsty from his run along the beach. Eventually, she brings him back up to the yard, greeted by Uncle Evan and Sondra, who are still chatting, leaning against the yard railing.

After a little while, Chelsea takes Rocket-Beau through the gate and back into his yard. Uncle Evan says goodbye to Sondra and Sondra disappears after Chelsea. Soon, I see Uncle Evan take off down the paddock on the quad bike, Jess and Bell tailing behind him. I stay in the tree a good while, and eventually I see Chelsea and Sondra come out of the milking shed, get in their car and head down the driveway. They don't see me watching them from my high perch.

Soon, June wanders over to the base of the fig tree. It seems June has grown tired of Callum and she wants to play with me now. I'm a bit tired and bored with sitting in the tree, so we make up a game. We imagine that the fig tree is an enormous palace and each tree limb is a separate room. We climb along the different branches and tell each other which room we've arrived in and what we'll do there.

'I'm in the music room and I'm playing the grand piano,' I announce.

Then June slides along a limb to the trunk of the tree, clinging on to it with her skinny arms and stepping out onto another limb. 'I'm in the kitchen and I'm baking a batch of chocolate brownies!' she yells.

I climb along branches enjoying the fantasy. At once, I'm in the bathroom, enjoying a long, hot, bubble bath. Then I'm in the library, surrounded by wall-to-wall bookshelves full of beautiful books. Eventually, I drop to the bottom of the tree, to explore my favourite place in this world of imagination; the stables. I pretend I'm roaming up the middle of an enormous stable, stopping at each stall to pat each one of my exquisite horses. There's the liver chestnut in the front stall. He's my dressage horse. Then there's the dappled grey. She's my show jumper. Then there's my palomino quarter-horse. I use him for trail riding.

The rain gets heavier, so we leave the fig tree and run across to one of the old sheds on the other side of the driveway. There's a rusty old car shell there. It has no tyres on it but there are seats in it and a steering wheel. We open the doors, wipe the dust and cobwebs off the seats and get in. The car smells awful, like dirt and wet carpet and grease. I'm in the driver's seat and June is in the front passenger seat. We pretend we're Mum and Dad. June looks out the window. She pretends to be putting lipstick on and adjusting her sunglasses in the rear-view mirror. I laugh at her clever impersonation of Mum.

I grab the steering wheel and pretend to be Dad, hands at ten and two, wearing a grumpy face and turning towards the backseat to rouse, 'Would you kids bloody shut up? Don't make me come back there!'

June laughs. 'That's just like Dad,' she tells me.

I face the front, twisting the steering wheel left and right, shifting the gearstick up and down and making revving noises from the base of my throat.

'I can see the beach!' shouts June. 'Who's ready for a swim?' she calls to the imaginary hoard of children crammed into the back seat.

I pretend to slow the car down, coming to a halt in the beach car park.

June and I sit there in silence for a while. The rain is coming down hard now, drumming against the tin roof, waterfalls cascading over the eaves.

'June,' I say suddenly. 'Do you like Mitchell?'

'Who?' Her face is blank.

'Mitchell,' I repeat. 'Cameron's friend?'

'Um…,' she ponders. 'What do you mean?'

'Forget about it,' I sigh.

'He's Cameron's friend,' she states, as though that explains her answer.

We sit quietly for a long time. Then I put my hand on her arm. 'I don't think Mitchell is very nice. I don't think you should…' But I stop. I'm not exactly sure what I want to say.

'You don't think I should what?'

'Just… play with him, I guess. I don't think you should play with him.'

'I don't. I don't play with him. He's Cameron's friend.'

'OK. Yeah. Well, if he wants to play with you, is what I'm saying. If he wants to play with you, just say no.'

'Why would he want to play with me?' She looks entirely perplexed. 'He's Cameron's friend,' she repeats.

'Well, if he ever… I dunno. Just stay away from him, OK?'

June says nothing. She has absolutely no idea what I'm going on about.

'OK?' I say a little louder.

She shrugs and lifts her eyebrows. 'OK,' she agrees, almost laughing at the strangeness of the conversation.

After a time, we leave the shed and wander back inside the house, kicking our shoes off and shaking the rain out of our hair like a couple of shaggy dogs.

The rain pummels all afternoon, the long hours stretching out lazily. We sit at the table and talk to Mum and Aunty Ruby and Debbie and we do some colouring in and we watch a bit of television and we eat shortbread biscuits and drink milk and it takes years to get to dinner time and it occurs to me that the boy's punishment of being bound to their room all afternoon was hardly fair at all. As June and I finally brush our teeth and trundle off to bed, it seems that we've spent the rainy day equally as incarcerated as Cameron and Mitchel.

*

I wake early to the sound of rain pelting on the roof. June snores softly beside me and when I get up to visit the outhouse, Uncle Evan is climbing into his boots. I ask him to wait while I get dressed for milking.

Uncle Evan isn't sure. 'Not today, Bridie. It's really coming down,' he tells me.

'Oh, please,' I beg.

He thinks for a good while but finally he relents. 'Just don't go getting a bloody cold,' he warns me. 'Your mother will kill me.'

In our gumboots and Drizabones, we trek across the sopping grass. Uncle Evan lets Jess and Bell off their chains and starts up the quad bike. We set off across the paddock and down towards the dam, where most of the Friesians are gathered, rumps turned against the blustering wind. The rain falls in heavy sheets and Uncle Evan cuts through puddle after puddle, water splashing up against the back of my Drizabone. Raindrops hang from my eyelashes and I lick my lips, relishing the sweet taste of summer rain.

As we near the cattle, Uncle Evan calls out commands to Jess and Bell, who round the mob and bark frantically, nipping at the heels of the heifers on the outside. One rogue cow ducks her head low, flaring her nostrils wide and threatening to take on Jess, but the dog barks loudly and rushes forward, the cow turning on her heels and falling into step with the mob. Soon, they're lumbering towards the dairy shed, legs paddling wide around their bloated udders, some of their teats already trickling with milk.

As the mob moves on, Uncle Evan notes a lone cow who's failed to join the herd. He calls out to Bell to come behind and the dog races out behind the quad bike and across to the beast, barking shrilly, but the dog's paws start sinking in the mud at the edge of the dam and she keeps changing direction, trying each time to track out a solid path towards the cow. Uncle Evan drives the quad bike nearer to the cow and now, from this perspective, it's plain to see the beast is bogged, more than knee-deep in the muddy quagmire between the dam and the grassy paddock.

Uncle Evan brings the bike to a standstill. He tells me to stay where I am and he picks his way across the grass and mud to get a better look at the cow. He tuts and swears and shakes his head and then he calls both Jess and Bell to come behind the beast and both dogs bound awkwardly across to the rear of the cow and with Uncle Evan calling out commands, they bark and bark at the cow, running from left to right.

The cow, assaulted from all sides, thrashes her head to and fro and bellows and moans and shifts the weight of her bulk in all directions but try as she might, she can't break free. Uncle Evan urges the dogs on, and soon they're sinking their sharp fangs into her rump and nipping at her ears. Bell sinks her teeth into the cow's nose and swings her body from side to side, shaking the cow's head frantically like a thrashing shark and flecks of blood are spattered across the white side of the cow's face. The cow bellows and moans, and now the rest of the herd has turned to watch the spectacle, one of their own sinking before them, and as her bellows grow more desperate the herd responds, the barrels of their bellies lifting each time they stretch their necks out long and call out to her. She bellows back, trying to shield her head against the dogs' onslaught. She struggles to lift her front legs out of the swamp but the slick black mud sucks at her skin and the more she squirms and wrestles, the deeper she sinks.

I'm a flood of tears. I scream to the dogs, 'No! Stop!' and Uncle Evan looks across at me, his face pulsing with fury. I fear he's about to release a torrent of reprimand in my direction but he catches himself.

He looks back to the bogged beast and shakes his head, calling the dogs off. It takes repeated commands to pull the dogs away. They keep returning to the stricken cow, biting her hind and her head and even swinging from her tail, frenzied foam frothing at their jowls that seem set, I'm sure, in a demonic grin. I am sobbing and sobbing and Uncle Evan returns to the bike and wraps his arms around me.

'Stop crying, Bridie,' he sighs. 'It's OK. We'll get these girls milked and then I'll get your dad to help me. We'll come and get her out.'

I struggle to collect myself, but when I look across at the cow, her head hung low, her sad eyes half shut, her nostrils flared and breathing hard, her ears and face patchy with her own bright blood, I convulse with fresh sobs. I fret the cow will die and I say so to Uncle Evan but he laughs and assures me the cow will be fine. He gets back on the bike and turns towards the mob, who are all standing with their heads facing the same direction, towards their sister cow.

'C'mon,' Uncle Evan roars, the vowel long and low, telling the dogs to get the mob moving, and reluctantly they turn towards the milking shed again, following the fence line towards the top of the paddock.

I watch Jess and Bell, both of them running too close to the hind legs of the cows, even nipping at their swaying bags of milk, still pumped from their frenzied attack on the stuck creature now behind us. I scowl at both of them and vow that I will never pat them again.

In the shed, I help Uncle Evan as best I can, filling the feed troughs and bringing the cows in and out when it's their turn to be hooked up to the metal suckers. I lay my hand on their warm, wet rumps and stroke them gently, trying to console them after their distressing ordeal. But all the while, my mind is with their sister cow, trapped in what I'm sure will become her muddy grave. I think I can hear her mournful moans floating up the hill, pleading to be reunited with her herd, wishing to be lazily munching on bran and pollard, the metal suckers alleviating the pressure from her bloated udders. Tears keep welling and spilling, welling and spilling, and Uncle Evan assures me more than once that the cow will be all right.

When the last heifer has been milked and returned to the paddock, I follow Uncle Evan into the house, where he tells Aunty Ruby and Debbie and my mum and dad about the bogged cow and he tells Dad to 'roll up your sleeves' and Dad borrows a pair of Uncle Evan's gum boots and a Drizabone and they both head out the door and I follow close behind them, almost tripping on Dad's heels, but Uncle Evan turns to me and barks, 'You're staying here, Bridie!' And I protest with more persistence than I usually dare but Dad, taking his cue from Uncle Evan, repeats the order. 'You stay up here in the house, Bridie! Don't you dare let us catch you near the dam,' and Aunty Ruby moves behind me and coaxes me over to the dining room table with promises of warm Milo and buttery toast and I watch the door slam shut behind the men and see their silhouettes through the window as they head off towards the shed. And while Aunty Ruby is putting bread in the toaster and turning the kettle on, I shift the curtains to the side and sneak a look and I can see that Uncle Evan and Dad are now walking towards the ute and Uncle Evan has a reel of thick, bright blue rope and he whistles to Jess and Bell, who launch themselves up onto the tray of the ute, and the ute starts with a shudder and they drive off towards the dam, Jess and Bell both wearing those maniacal grins.

And even though I'm soaked through and shivering and the Milo is steaming and the toast smells delicious, I can't eat anything. I can't answer Aunty Ruby or Mum or Debbie when they try to distract me with questions and change the subject away from Uncle Evan and Dad. Instead, I just sit at the dining room table, my tummy a squirmy mess of sadness and fear as I picture one end of that bright blue rope wrapped around the head of the stuck cow and the other end attached to the ute and Uncle Evan revving the ute hard and tugging at the cow as the dogs dig into her rear and she roars and pants and thrashes about and for the life of me I can't shake the image from my head of the cow's barrel body being ripped clean from her legs and dragged along behind the ute while her black and white stumps stay firmly fixed in the sucking mud, pumping fountains of bright red blood as her tongue lolls flaccidly and her head releases one final, desperate moan.

I stay seated at the dining room table watching June and Callum play with one of Callum's puzzles and watching Debbie nursing baby Alex and listening to Mum and Aunty Ruby talk about which of Aunty Ruby's pot plants are looking happy and I suspect I'll spend forever in this cell of mental torment but before long the back door opens and in comes Dad and Uncle Evan. Both men wriggle out of their Drizabones and kick off their mud-caked boots and wipe at their mud-smeared faces and I look up at Uncle Evan expectantly but he doesn't say anything. He simply smiles at me and squeezes my shoulder and without even asking, I dive into my boots and fly out the door.

I shoot across the spongy, soggy grass and go behind the outhouse and pick my way along the fence line down the hill towards the mob that is gathered around the dam and I run so fast that I stumble a couple of times, almost toppling over myself but I press on and I reach the herd and scan the beasts looking for the long-suffering wretch that has occupied my thoughts this entire morning. I see the deep tracks where the wheels of the ute have spun against the weight of the bogged cow and I see the deep impressions left by the legs of the bogged cow and I search the mob and see the bogged cow, now free from the bog but coated up to her belly in dark, tar-like sludge and I search her face for signs of trauma and I ready myself to wrap my arms around her neck and whisper quiet words of comfort in her ear. But as I near her, she bucks a little on her hind legs and swings around. Then she quietly lowers her head to sniff at the lush green grass, wrapping her tongue around a tuft and effortlessly ripping it out, munching dopily.

9

The rain clears by lunchtime and it's decided that in the afternoon we will visit the blowhole. We always visit the blowhole when we come to see Aunty Ruby and Uncle Evan. There's a surf beach near the blowhole, so we all get dressed in swimmers and Mum and Debbie organise an esky with drinks and snacks and beers for the men and the boys get their fishing gear ready. Cameron and Mitchell are allowed out of their room today but the grown-ups are still well angry at their firecracker stunt and both boys tread carefully and say very little.

Aunty Ruby and Uncle Evan and Debbie and Callum and Alex travel in Debbie's car, Aunty Ruby tucked into the backseat between Callum's car seat and Alex's capsule. We follow their car down the drive, all of us in our usual spots, and even though I don't want to be sitting next to Mitchell, I sense for the first time that he would rather not be sitting next to me either. He keeps his legs pressed together and makes an effort to move across the seat, as far away from me as possible so that he's almost sitting on top of Cameron, and Cameron even tells him, 'Hey, shove over.' And I suppose I should be happy about it but I just feel sad and confused and spend the whole drive to the blowhole wondering what it was that I did wrong and I guess it all has something to do with being 'frigid'.

We all pile out of the car and follow the winding path that leads to the blowhole. June and I run on ahead, eager to see the volcanic explosions of foam and to hear the roar of the ocean, rolling and receding and smashing its way through the mouth of the rock. We wander out as far as we dare, salty spray misting up our faces, making us purse our lips tight to stop the brine from touching our tongues. We kneel on the rock and lower ourselves as close as we can to the blowhole. And it occurs to me that I haven't seen the blowhole since this time last year. And that whole time, it's been right here, doing exactly what it's doing right now, rumbling and exploding and rumbling and exploding and I wonder how many times it spurts up like this every day. I wonder how many times it's exploded since the last time we visited it and I ask my dad this question and Dad says, 'Well, count how many times it spurts in a minute and then multiply that by sixty and then multiply that by...' and he keeps talking but it sounds too much like mind-boggling mathematics so I stop listening. Instead, I move even closer to the blowhole until Mum and Aunty Ruby shriek at me to get back before I 'fall right through!'

After a while, we walk back along the winding path and make our way down the walkway towards the surf beach. There's a grassy area where Dad and Uncle Evan dump the heavy esky and Mum and Aunty Ruby and Debbie settle on the concrete table and chairs, where they can keep an eye on us in the water without getting sand in their shoes. There's a little play area where Callum can climb a rope tower and Debbie can push him on the swings.

We eat watermelon and crackers with French onion dip. We drink plastic cups of lemonade, fizzy and ice cold after sitting in the esky. The sun is hot and the air is steamy after all the heavy rain. Aunty Ruby bounces baby Alex on her knee, a little white bucket hat protecting his face from the sun. June and I are keen to strip our clothes off and enter the surf and we're down there, dancing over and ducking under waves before the boys have even set up their fishing gear.

June and I play our usual games. Handstands and tumble turns and talking under water. And being here with June, laughing and singing and talking in the language only we can understand, the hours roll away with the tide. In all that time, I hardly think about Mitchell, or Debbie, or Chelsea and Rocket-Beau or the bogged cow. The waves caress my sick, scared tummy and by the time Mum calls us back to shore, our shadows long and lean across the flat, hard sand, I'm feeling something close to me again.

On the way home, we buy fish and chips for dinner, all of us kids salivating at the vinegary aroma filling the car, our stomachs twisted inside out with hunger. When we're finally back at Uncle Evan's and Aunty Ruby's, Dad and Uncle Evan crack open a couple of beers and Aunty Ruby and Mum sip from their slender peach-coloured bottles and we kids flock like seagulls around the chips, blowing on them and greedily popping them into our mouths and Mum announces that it was a lovely way to spend the last afternoon of our South Coast holiday.

My head shoots up, hot chip frozen in midair. 'What do you mean?' I say.

'What do you mean, what do I mean?' says Mum.

'Are we going home tomorrow?' I ask.

'We are,' says Mum. 'We can't stay here forever, love. I think Aunty Ruby and Uncle Evan would probably like their house back.'

'But I haven't…' I start. But I don't know what to say. I want to say that I haven't had a sleepover with Samantha or I haven't had my make-up done by Debbie or I haven't had a ride on Rocket-Beau but it seems no matter how long we stay, there doesn't seem much chance of any of these things happening anyway.

A heavy weight descends and my shoulders sag beneath it. I'm not ready to go home. Going home means Dad will be going back to work. Going home means that Cameron can probably go to work with Dad but June and I will be stuck at home with Mum.

There's nothing left to say. Everyone settles in. The fish and chips are gone and Mum wraps the half-squeezed lemons in the greasy paper and puts them in the bin. Dad and Uncle Evan have another beer and Aunty Ruby gets the cards down from the top of the fridge, dealing out measured piles around the table. Cameron and Mitchell are invited to play and they take their seats next to the grown-ups as June and Callum disappear down the hall.

I don't want to sit around watching everybody play cards. I don't want to follow June and Callum up the hall. I quietly sidle over to the back door, don a pair of boots and slip outside.

It's dusk. Pink. Soft. A crow squarks nearby. The cat, sitting in the middle of the cracked path, scurries beneath the house. The breeze tickles my face and I push my rogue curls behind my ears.

I set out across the squishy grass, headed nowhere in particular. I turn left, leaving the row of leadlight windows near the back door behind me and I step up onto the veranda. I round the house, running my hand along the rough brick exterior. My boots make clunking sounds on the wooden decking beneath me, and as I reach each window, I tap, tap, tap with my knuckles, listening to the glassy thud.

I reach the other side of the house, jump off the veranda and walk to the fig tree. I place my hands on the tree's trunk, run them over the names of my brother and cousins etched in its flesh and it takes little imagination to feel a pulse, throbbing in the heart of the tree. I search around, find a sharp rock on the ground and start carving again, this time determined to carve my name into the trunk, grunting with each stroke in a bid to make my mark, and finally it's there, BRIDIE, in chunky, untidy block letters.

I walk around the tree and stand at the top of the driveway. Down the dusty road to my left is Samantha's house. I discover I can no longer picture Samantha on her own. In my mind, she always has her arm around the stupid boy's waist, her hand on his chest, a smug grin on her face. I suppose they're both down there now, at the end of that dusty road, snuggling up on the couch watching some evening program that I'm probably still too young to watch.

I turn around. I see Jess and Bell. They're both inside their drum kennels. I can see their noses poking out, resting on their front paws. I walk past the dogs. But I don't pat them. I keep walking straight ahead. I reach the milking shed door, and go in.

I take the deepest breath, my senses flooded with the smell of cow and lucerne and bran and milk. I walk past the silver vat, through the main room of the milking sheds with its feed crushes and metal suckers, and out the other side to Rocket-Beau's yard.

Rocket-Beau is facing away from me. He twists his long neck

around as I approach and then he slowly turns around and steps towards me, his enormous head bobbing and swaying with each step. I stretch my hand out towards his muzzle and he snorts noisily. Once again, I have no treat, but I bend down and pick a bunch of long grass from this side of the yard and he accepts it greedily.

And I decide, then and there, even though I didn't know it before this second, I decide I'm going to ride this horse.

I bob my head down and slip through the railings. I sidle up close to Rocket-Beau. I press my cheek against his warm wither and gather up a bunch of his mane in my hand. I whisper to him, 'Easy, boy,' and run my hand along his wide chest and silky foreleg.

I wander over to Rocket-Beau's shed and see that his tack is still there. Without even thinking about it, I lift the saddle from its pommel, the saddle rug resting on top of it. I bring it out into the yard and place it on the ground next to Rocket-Beau. I lift the saddle rug, shaking it gently and placing it on Rocket-Beau's back. I keep talking to him quietly, soothingly, 'Easy, boy,' although he barely stirs. He stands there patiently as I lift the saddle, struggling awkwardly to hoist it up onto my own shoulder and then push it up and onto his back. The saddle rug gets pushed off his back and around the other side of him, and I have to put the saddle back down, duck beneath his head and retrieve the saddle rug and duck back under his head and start again.

Eventually, I have the saddle on his back and I go around the other side to untwist the girth and then back again to pull the girth beneath Rocket-Beau's belly and buckle it up. I grunt and grimace and pull it as tight as I can but when I've buckled it up and I wriggle the saddle around to check that it's tight it swivels around loosely. I try Chelsea's trick, kneeing Rocket-Beau in the belly to make him breathe out while I try to tighten the girth but I can't make it reach the next hole in the belt. I decide it will have to do.

I go back to the shed and find Rocket-Beau's bridle. I've never put a saddle on a horse before but I'm guessing that it's easier than putting on a bridle. I take forever to decide which bits of leather go over the ears and which bits go around his nose. I lift the bridle up over his ears but my actions surprise him and Rocket-Beau flinches and pulls his head away and I have to gently coax him back to me, saying his name and clicking my tongue.

Finally, I get the pieces of leather around his head but the metal bit that should be in his mouth is actually behind his mouth, pinching at the soft skin of his muzzle. I remember that Chelsea actually put the bit in his mouth first before lifting the bridle over his head, so I take it off again and try to put the bit in his mouth, and he opens his mouth and takes it easily and I've got it in right, but then I let go of the bit to gather up the rest of the bridle again and then Rocket-Beau keeps his mouth open and the bit falls out and the whole bridle is on the ground.

I pick up the bridle and put it on like I did the first time. The bit isn't in his mouth. It's behind his muzzle and hanging quite loosely, but the leather straps around his ears hold and I separate the reins and stand on tip-toes to toss the reins over his head.

My heart is racing and my stomach flutters. I'm talking to the horse, saying his name over and over, rhythmically, hypnotically, more to calm my nerves than his.

And then June speaks. 'What are you doing?'

Once again, she's snuck up on me, and I'm annoyed that she's frightened me. 'Geez, June!'

'What are you doing?' she asks again.

'Nothing,' I say. Which is, of course, a ridiculous thing to say.

'It doesn't look like nothing,' she tells me. 'It looks like you're about to ride this horse.'

I sigh. 'Well,' I start. 'It was meant to be a surprise.'

'What do you mean?' she asks.

'Well, after I saddled him up, I was going to come and get you. Don't you want to ride the horse?'

Of course, I'm not at all keen to let June ride the horse. But I have no chance of swearing her to secrecy if I don't implicate her in my crime.

'Shouldn't Uncle Evan be here?' she wants to know.

'June,' I say, 'do you want to ride the horse or not?'

At first, her face is hard to read. She seems dubious, squinting her eyes and chewing her lip, but then a grin breaks across her features and she's nodding her head. 'Yes!' She jumps a little and claps her hands. 'Yes! I want to ride the horse!'

'OK, well,' I say, 'you need to promise me that you'll listen to me and do everything I say, OK?'

She nods and follows my instructions as I tell her to slip through the rail and stand beside me. I tell her that she needs to place her foot in the stirrup and I hold it out for her, but Rocket-Beau is tall and the stirrup is far too high for June to get her thonged foot anywhere near it. Instead, I try to lift her up, wrapping my arms around her hips and thrusting her towards the saddle, but still it's too high, and my legs falter and my arms give out and both of us tumble in the dirt and Rocket-Beau lifts his head up and pins his ears back and takes a few side steps away from us.

June is having second thoughts now. She senses Rocket-Beau is unsettled and she tells me she's not sure she wants to have a ride after all, but I hush her quickly and tell her everything will be OK. I tell her I have a new plan. I decide that June will have to reach the saddle by climbing to the top rail of the fence.

'It'll be easy,' I tell her. 'You sit yourself on the top rail there and I'll hold Rocket-Beau's reins and you step across into the saddle and then I'll walk you around his yard holding on to his reins, OK? It'll be fun!'

She's not smiling and she doesn't seem excited, but June does what I say. She climbs up to the top rung on the fence and I walk Rocket-Beau around so that he's right up close to the fence. It's hard to get him to walk when I ask him because the bridle bit is hanging loosely and I don't have much control over his head, but I'm able to get him up close to the fence and I tell June to put her left foot in the stirrup and jump across onto the saddle.

June gingerly places her foot in the left stirrup and Rocket-Beau lifts his head and snorts a little, and I'm scared he's about to move, so I tell June, 'Quickly! Jump!' and she reacts to my panicked tone and she jumps and her left foot is in the stirrup and she scrambles to hitch her right leg up and over the seat of the saddle. But June's weight is in her left leg. The saddle is too loose. It yanks to the side and Rocket-Beau snorts and rears up and I'm thrown backwards, on my bottom, on my hands, in the dirt, and June screams out and the saddle is still done up but it's slipped halfway around Rocket-Beau's belly. June is struggling to get off but her left foot is now positioned at a strange angle, stuck there in the stirrup.

'Get off!' I tell her, but she can't.

Her foot is stuck in the stirrup and Rocket Beau whips his body around and June swings with him and her head cracks back against the hard dirt, a terrible sound, and her body goes limp and loose, like a floppy doll, like a pair of Mum's stockings, floating in the breeze on the washing line. Rocket-Beau rears again and June's body flips up and down again, his hooves stomping on her leg, another crack to the head and I'm screaming, not words, not aimed at the horse or my sister, just screaming, wildly, trapped in a seemingly endless moment of terror.

And then I shout the word, 'God! Please, God!' and Rocket-Beau has four legs on the ground now and the saddle has rotated completely, the seat of it right underneath his belly and the stirrup is on the ground and June's foot slips out easily and she lies there, still, on the dirt, her body twisted at odd angles, a mess of blood and dirt, almost black, on the side of her face.

Rocket-Beau is snorting and whinnying and dancing, his front hooves lifting quickly up and down and his back leg lashing out, kicking at some invisible thing behind him until he finally brings his head down low and comes to a standstill, his flanks twitching, his nostrils flared, a long, loud snort.

I'm trembling. I'm crying so hard I can't close my mouth and saliva is dangling from my chin. I wipe my mouth and taste the dirt and I try to speak but I can't make my mouth work. I want to move to June but

I'm frightened to touch her and when I finally do, I'm convinced she's cold and she looks blue and I watch her chest but I see no rise or fall and I'm so, so sick that I can taste the fish and chips coming up from my stomach. I look at Rocket-Beau, just standing there. I look towards the house and I picture the grown-ups inside, laughing, playing card games and drinking beers. I look for the sun but it's slunk behind the highway. Everything is quiet, just the sound of my hacking sobs and my heartbeat throbbing in my ears.

And from somewhere, not so far away, the sleepy caw of a crow.

10

I'm running. I've slipped through the railings of Rocket-Beau's yard and I'm running. It's hard to run because it's hard to breath while I'm still sobbing, my mouth frozen in a twisted gaping hole, but I'm running.

I run along the fence line, down the hill and past the dam. The cows are dotting the grassy pasture. I see the bogged cow there, so stupid, her legs still caked, standing there near the gluggy black mud that almost swallowed her, dopily chewing her cud.

I run all the way around the dam and across the paddock. I'm dodging ditches and potholes and hurdling over low bushes and I run forever until I hit the fence.

This is as far as I've ever been. On the other side of this fence line is the base of the hill. I stand at the fence, placing my hands on the top rung, feeling the sharp barbs penetrate the fleshy heels of my palms and I'm breathing so hard I can barely hear a sound over my own gasping. My heartbeat drums at my ears. I look to the left, towards the highway, a single line of tiny cars snaking their way along the horizon. I look to my right, back up the hill towards the house, Rocket-Beau still standing there, the saddle underneath his belly, June cold and blue, lying crooked in the dirt.

I'm in so much trouble. I've never been in this much trouble.

I climb the fence. I try to stomp the fence down with my boot but the rungs spring up and snatch at my thighs, snaring my shorts and nicking bits of flesh, drawing blood. I scramble to the other side of the fence, stand there a moment, catching my breath. A strange feeling washes over me now. I seem to be floating. I can't feel the ground beneath my feet. My hands and face are tingling and my entire body feels light. My boots feel strangely heavy on the ends of my legs. For a while, I wonder if perhaps I'm asleep. I'm dreaming. Or sleepwalking, stuck somewhere between wake and sleep. But I know it's not a dream. I know June is up there. I can see the blood. And the stillness. And I know it's not a dream.

I walk across the flat base of the hill. I look up, to the top of the hill. I've never seen it from this angle, from so near. When I've looked at the hill from the veranda of the house, it's always looked enormous, but here, at the foot of the hill, it seems monstrous. But I know that tonight I'm going to climb over this hill.

One step. Left. Then another. Right. One foot. Then the other. I've lost the urge to run. I'm tired now. Strangely so. My legs are wobbly and my breathing is slowing down. Time feels thin. Stretched. And I move as though I'm walking into the wind, trudging through sand.

The sun has bled out. The night sky is lighting up with stars and I fret for June, alone in the dark. Don't think, I tell myself. Just walk. Don't think. It gets harder to see where I'm going and the scrub is thick. There are brambles whipping at my legs that are covered in gashes and welts. One step, then another. One step, then another. Again and again, I pace out a track but find my path is barricaded by impenetrable brambles and I have to stop, back up, and find a new way. I step backwards and sideways and forwards and sideways, sometimes stumbling over. My hands are raw and I press the heels of my palms together in a bid to press away the pain. My breathing is so heavy now, ripping at my throat. My chest is sore and my face, my torso, even my legs are filmed with sweat. Suddenly, I panic that snakes might be here, in the scrub, and I bring each foot down heavier, stomping the ground hard hoping to scare them away.

When it seems I've walked for ages, I stop and look behind me. The house is certainly far away. I can make out the roof and the veranda, lights glowing in the windows. I can just see the outhouse and the fig tree. But I look up, to the top of the hill, and I know I'm not halfway up. Not even a quarter of the way up. I put my head down and keep walking. One foot. Left. Then another. Right.

I don't think about anything other than getting to the top of the hill. The incline is so steep I'm not really walking any more. I'm climbing, on all fours, my hands stretched out in front of me, seeking purchase on the boulders or thick tufts of grass before lifting my foot high and bringing it down again in front of me. Climbing stairs. I'm startled once by a rabbit, hiding still until I'm almost on top of it, darting out from underneath me and zigzagging across the side of the hill.

When I guess I'm maybe halfway up, I turn around and look back at the house. It's impossible to see the milking shed, the outhouse or the fig tree in the dark. Lights glow from within the house but it's too far away to make out whether anyone is outside in the yard.

It's completely dark now, and fear turns to terror. The air, windy up here, is full of monsters. I'm certain one is lurking behind every bush. I can picture their demonic faces, jagged teeth and slimy skin, claws thrashing at me in the dark, carving my face up, slicing my throat. My body is so tired, my jelly legs are burning, but I'm too afraid to stop. I need to move, away from the farm, away from the monsters. I climb and climb. I climb for so long I wonder whether morning will crack soon, but the darkness holds and I don't stop. I need to reach the sea.

In my mind, so many times, I've imagined walking over this hill. I've imagined reaching the summit in one monumental step, all at once seeing the ocean laid out before me, angelic voices singing Alleluia! But that's not what happens now. It's too dark. Although the sky is sprayed with stars, there's hardly any light, the moon a fingernail clipping hanging over the highway. Instead, I notice that the climbing finally gets easier, the ground seems to level out. The wind is stronger still and although I can't see the ocean, I can hear it. The gentle ebb and flow of the waves, the water folding over itself.

I walk towards the sound, but in an instant I lose my footing. The ground disappears beneath me. I squeal and throw my body backwards, landing with a thud so hard it pumps the wind out of me. I realise I'm on the edge of a cliff.

There has to be a way down to the beach. Cameron and Mitchell have walked over this hill and have swum in the ocean and walked back again. There has to be a way down. But it's too dark and too dangerous and I can't tell where the ground stays firm or falls away and I'm too scared to turn in any direction now and I sit there on the ground in a winded heap and I bring my head down to the ground and curl up in a ball as tightly as I can and I tune in to the lullaby of the ocean and I will sleep to come and rock me so gently in its arms that I never, never wake up again.

*

Hours pass, but sleep doesn't come. Shivering with cold, I lie awake, my belly swimming, the skin on my arms lifting off the bone. There's a picture now, on a loop. It's June, her body flicking like the ribbon of a gymnast, the crunching smack of her head against the hard dirt. It plays over and over, each time the sound sending waves like an electric shock through my body.

I try to push the scene away from my mind, try to push it down and concentrate on my breathing, but it brews and swells and then explodes, projecting again and again onto the screen in my brain. Like a floodlight. Like a lightning strike. Like a punch to the chest. Like a stab to the heart. Each time I sense it coming, I feel my body tightening up, bracing itself against the terror.

I try to think of something else. In my mind's eye, I stand up and back away from June's broken body. I walk backwards, away from the yard, back through the milking shed, back across the spongy grass in front of the outhouse. And back inside the house.

I picture the scene inside the house. Dad and Uncle Evan drinking beers, Mum and Aunty Ruby sipping on their peach-coloured bubbles, Cameron and Mitchell holding their card hands close to their chests. Debbie sitting at the table, her new baby wrapped snuggly and rocking gently in her arms.

I'm scared of my mum. My dad. I'm scared of all of them. I'm scared of what will happen when they learn what I've done. For a time,

I stand silently in the corner, unnoticed, and watch the scene, but then, in my mind's eye, my mum looks at me. I don't need to speak. She can read my face. In my mind's eye, she stands up, dropping her drink, bringing her hands to her face, cupping them over her mouth, a look of total horror. She moves towards the door, soon followed by Dad, then Uncle Evan and Aunty Ruby. I try to scream. I try to move towards the door, to stop them from exiting, but I'm speechless, frozen still. Cameron and Mitchell have dropped their card hands and are following the adults out the door. My mind's eye floats above them, watching them race across the grass, pile through the milking shed and arrive at Rocket-Beau's yard.

When they reach the yard, they squirm through the railings and crowd around my sister's lifeless body. I can't even see June from up here, her figure hidden by the back of the heads of the grown-ups that are crouched around her. But then I see my mum, her body straightening up and reeling back, calling out, a tortured, grief-stricken howl. Her face is stretched unnaturally. She places one hand on the side of her face, another on her stomach. Her body bends at the waist, folds and crumples.

And I know, for certain, I have no family now. My mother will never forgive me for this. My father will want to kill me. My brother will never speak to me again. Uncle Evan and Aunty Ruby will never again welcome me to the farm. I will be disowned. By all of them.

I have no family. I have no home.

The wind is cruel and full of howling monsters. I hug my body tight, burying my face into the crook of my arms. The ocean rears and collapses. A few times, I nod off briefly, but nightmarish visions keep ripping me out of slumber. I hold a baby in my arms, my breasts huge and exposed, enormous nipples leaking with milk. The baby suckles and I look at her face and I realise it's June. My breasts change colour, ashen and grey, threaded with black veins. My milk turns black, seeping out between June's tiny lips and trickling down the side of her face.

In another vision, I see June in the back seat of the car. I sit on one side of her and Mitchell is on the other. I watch his hand move along her leg, creep inside her shorts. I look at June's face and she's laughing. When I wake, my eyes are wet.

Eventually, the dark is smeared with a faint light as the sun begins to shimmer across the surface of the sea. I sit up and see the ocean now and I can see that I was right. I'm almost perched on the edge of a cliff. To my left, only metres away, there is a cut-out stairway that leads down to the beach. I stand, take the stairs and walk down to the shore.

I take my boots off and let the cold water wash over my feet. It's icy and stings my heels and my toes that are covered with blisters. I bend down and cup the foamy water in my hands, splashing it over my face. My eyes are stinging, my head is heavy, my body aches. I'm parched, so thirsty my tongue seems stuck to the roof of my mouth and I'm struck by the absurdity of being surrounded by so much water that I'm unable to drink. The beach is completely deserted. I know that this is not a popular beach, not a surf beach. There are never any lifeguards or flags here. There aren't even any early morning surfers. I walk across the wet sand to the end of the beach, where the rocks and the cliff face make it impossible to go any further, and I turn and sit and watch the ocean and the deserted beach and I listen to the waves and I think about June.

It is my earliest memory. My hand is in my father's hand. He holds a bunch of brightly coloured flowers in the other. We walk down the corridor of a hospital, the stench of disinfectant thick in the air. I hear the blips and beeps of hospital machines. We near a door and Dad slows down, rounding the corner and then I see my mum, sitting up in the bed, a white hospital gown hanging loosely around her shoulders. My father leans in to kiss my mother on the forehead. Cameron is already sitting on the edge of the bed. And beside the bed, a clear, plastic crib.

My baby sister. Wrapped in a stripey blanket. Smaller than a doll. Her hair a shock of black. Her face heart-shaped. Her lips a tiny 'O'.

I sit on the end of the bed as my dad lifts my baby sister out of the crib and places her in my arms. He tells me to be careful to hold her head up. And I am. I am careful with my precious baby sister. I nurse her so gently and say her name, softly, and Dad tells me to look up and smile at the camera.

When June comes home, she sleeps in my room. She's in a cot at first, but soon we both sleep in single beds with matching quilt covers and Holly Hobby wallpaper all over the walls. We talk at night when the lights are turned off. We get up early in the morning and creep down the hallway, careful not to wake Mum and Dad. We make Milo and watch cartoons, sitting almost on top of the television. Santa visits, leaving presents in pillowcases at the end of our beds. I have a Strawberry Shortcake doll. She blows strawberry-scented kisses when I press her soft tummy. June has a lifelike doll with hazel eyes and silky hair that drinks from a bottle and needs her nappy changed. There's a white toy box in the corner of our room. One morning, I use the lid as a slippery dip, cracking it in the middle, and June races to tell Mum what has happened, eager to incriminate me and plead her own innocence.

June starts kindergarten. I've already been at school for a couple of years and I'm the protective big sister. I walk her to her classroom, show her around the playground, point out the toilets and the tuck shop, show her which bubbler has the best water pressure. One day, she loses a lacy red purse and I take her to the front office, speaking for her, explaining what has happened. After school, June and I race out the gate to find Mum waiting with all the other mothers and we all walk home, June and I kicking at stones, playing I-spy and singing songs we learnt at school.

On the weekends, June and I need nothing but each other. We play imaginary games. Schoolteachers. Shops. Hairdressers. Doctors. We spend hours cutting newspapers into tiny pieces and jumping underneath our makeshift snow. We play records on Dad's turntable and make up synchronised dance moves like the dancers we see on *Countdown*. In the summer time, we ride our bikes around the streets wearing denim shorts and bikini tops, swimming in the backyard pools of kids we just met, mindful of Mum's warning to be home before the streets lights come on.

I have no memory before June. My sleepless night curled up on the edge of the cliff is my first night ever away from her. And then the tears come. Shuddering sobs that rob my chest of air.

I've never felt so afraid. My body trembles and hums. It seems like I'm almost hovering above the ground. Above my body. By the time the sun is high in the sky, I feel like I've gone mad with thirst. I think myself in circles. What should I do? Where should I go? How will I find water to drink? Food to eat? But I don't move. I sit in the sand, my back up against the cliff face and watch the sun crawl across the sky.

In the afternoon, I'm sleepy. I rest my head on my knees and close my eyes, but sleep won't come. I'm suddenly surprised by a figure at the end of the beach. A man. Barefooted. Blue shorts and a white T-shirt. He throws a stick for a shaggy brown dog who follows it into the water and drags it back up the beach. He walks my way. I feel the urge to run, to hide, but there's nowhere to go and in no time he's too close. Within earshot.

'Hello,' he calls.

His dog bounds towards me, stops briefly to sniff my hand then bounces off towards the water.

'Hello,' I say.

He tilts his head, moving closer. 'Are you all right?'

'Yes, thank you. I'm fine.'

After a while he says, 'Where's your mum? Your dad?'

'Um….' I point towards the stairs, cut out of the side of the cliff. 'They're coming soon,' I tell him.

He looks at the stairs. He looks back at me. I feel his eyes move over my dirty shorts, my scratched-up legs, my blistered feet.

Finally, he says, 'Are you sure you're OK?'

'Uh-huh,' I nod.

'OK, well….if you're sure…' And he whistles to his dog and turns around, gradually disappearing down the other end of the beach.

11

I spend all afternoon sitting up against the rocks, watching the ocean, listening to the waves, and nobody else visits the beach. Occasionally, I walk down to the water, wash my feet, my hands and face. And I walk back to the rock. The sun slinks slowly over the grassy dunes on top of the cliff and I lay my head down in the sand. And I try, I try so hard, not to think.

But it doesn't work. Images assault me, a mashed-up storm over which I have no control, each vision swirling in a tornado of colours. And sounds. And smells. And thoughts. And feelings. I'm in the car, staring out the window with the hot wind slapping my hair against my face, my dad at the wheel, my mum beside him. I'm on the back seat, sitting next to Mitchell, his hand pressing my hand into him. I'm on the front porch of Samantha's house, the door slamming in my face. I'm on the beach, knee-deep in the water, reeling my fish in, Dad's face an angry grimace. I'm in the cupboard, watching Debbie cry, feeding her baby. I'm on the rocks, watching the fisherman and wondering whether Callum is lost forever. I'm climbing the fig tree, too high, stuck, and crying out for help. I'm in the old car shell, the smell of grease and dust, wiping cobwebs off my face. I'm in the chook house, trying to pluck an egg from underneath a mass of feathers with a sharp beak. I'm in the dairy shed, watching the dopey cows munch lazily on breakfast. I'm in the round yard, watching Chelsea canter about on Rocket-Beau. I'm in the big bed, next to June, watching cars climb the highway in the dark. I'm at the dam, watching Jess and Bell hanging off the nose of the bogged cow by their fangs. I'm at the bottom of the driveway, swinging on Uncle Evan's gate. I'm at the table, crying over a plate of flathead. I'm at the blowhole, falling into the volcanic opening and rolling away with the current. I'm at the dining room table, scoffing scone after scone, the jam sticky on my mouth. I'm under the Christmas tree, its pine perfume clouding the house. I'm in the bath with June and Callum, splashing and shrieking. I'm in the dark at the top of the cliff, hiding from monsters and praying for sleep.

And this is how I spend the afternoon, stuck on a carousel, willing the pictures away and praying for sleep.

And finally, I do. I finally fall asleep.

*

From somewhere up the other end of the beach, I hear a faint sound. It's completely dark, but when I look towards the direction of the sound I see a light beam slicing through the dark. At first, I think it's Mitchell, or Cameron, come to find me, playing Murder in the Dark. But then I remember. I remember where I am. I remember June, and Rocket-Beau, and the dam and the hill and the cliff and the beach. And I sit up, shake my head awake.

I squint my eyes and I can tell, by the way it's cutting through the dark at different angles, I can tell that it's a torch. Two torches, chopping in and out and criss-crossing over each other. And they're coming closer. I rub at my eyes. And then I hear a voice.

'Bridie! Briiiiiiiidieeeeee!'

A second voice joins in. 'Bridie! Where are you? Bridie?'

It's Uncle Evan. And my dad. I try to call out. I open my mouth and make a strange sound, but my mouth is too dry, my tongue like glue. I'm crying, quietly, and the flashlights are moving closer and the voices are getting louder, always calling out the same thing.

'Bridie! Bridie! Bridie!'

Then one of the flashlights is upon me. It's coming closer, slicing around in the night sky and then a huge hand is on my shoulder, pulling me to my feet. Uncle Evan.

'I've got her!' he shouts. 'Over here! I've got her!'

Two strong hands are hooking me under the arms and lifting me up, both my feet off the ground and my torso slung over his shoulder.

'I've got you, Bridie,' he says. 'I've got you.'

And all I can do is cry. I want to say I'm sorry and my mouth struggles to push the words out, 'I'm sorry,' but Uncle Evan pats me on the back and tells me to 'sssshhhhhhhh' and I bury my face in his neck and my face is wet with tears and my sobs are hacking and then my dad is there, taking my whole body in his arms and asking, 'Are you all right? Are you all right?' and I'm about to tell Uncle Evan and Dad again that I'm so sorry, I'm so sorry that June is dead.

But then my dad sets me down on the ground and takes my face in his rough hands and he yells at me, 'What the hell were you thinking, Bridie? The both of you could have been killed!'

I don't understand. And they are the first words I say. 'I don't understand.'

'What don't you understand?' He's angry, shouting. 'What don't you understand about doing what you're bloody told?'

But those words are bouncing around my brain – 'both of you could have been killed'.

And now I'm crying so hard I can barely stand. 'June's alive?' I sob, incredulous.

My mind can barely comprehend this. June is alive. My baby sister is alive. It seems impossible. The little girl I saw flung around the horse yard, the head I heard crack against the ground, the body I saw crumpled, cold and blue in the yard. It seems impossible that she's alive.

But now, it seems, she is.

*

I'm shivering, and Dad has wrapped his jacket around my shoulders. He and Uncle Evan walk beside me, one on each side of me, and they half carry me and half drag me along the beach, all the way back to the other end, where the sand dunes lead up to a grassy flat. We go through a gate in the fence line and walk over to Uncle Evan's ute, which is parked on the side of the road.

Dad helps me up into the middle of the bench seat and hops in beside me. The clock on the dashboard says one fifteen. It's warm in the ute and after a minute I'm not shivering so much any more. But I'm near dying from thirst.

'Is there any water?' I ask.

Dad picks up a drink bottle from the floor on the passenger side. He unscrews the lid and hands it to me. I guzzle it back, emptying the entire contents of the bottle and still so thirsty.

'I suppose you're hungry too,' says Dad. 'You'll have to wait till we get home.'

But I'm not hungry. Warm relief is swimming through my body. June is alive. And I'm not hungry.

Uncle Evan starts the ute, the headlights bursting onto the stretch of road ahead. He looks at me and shakes his head. And I want to know. I want to ask them what happened to June. I want to know how she is, but Dad and Uncle Evan are somber and silent and I crouch down in my seat and don't say anything.

We head off down the highway, then take the laneway that takes us to the bottom of Uncle Evan's driveway. For the first time since I can remember, it's Dad who gets out and opens the gate, shutting it behind us and getting back in the ute before we head up to the house.

Uncle Evan pulls up on the other side of the fig tree and I follow him and Dad out of the car. I can see the lights are on through the kitchen window.

Dad opens the back door and calls out, 'We've got her,' and I follow him inside to see Aunty Ruby, Debbie, Cameron and Mitchell sitting around the dining room table.

'Sweet Jesus,' says Aunty Ruby, and I can't read the expression on her face but she crosses the room to hold me. 'Bridie,' she says, pulling me in. 'Bridie, Bridie.' And then, turning to Dad, 'Where was she?'

And Dad tells them where they found me. Aunty Ruby looks at me and shakes her head.

And I look around the table, at Debbie, at Cameron, at Mitchell, at Dad and Uncle Evan, and I wait for someone to speak but no one says anything and I whisper, 'Where's Mum?'

And Dad tells me she's exactly where she has been for the past twenty-four hours. At the hospital with June. And Dad looks at me a long, long time. He turns to Uncle Evan and says, 'Call the police, will you? Tell them we've found her. I'm heading back to the hospital.' Then he turns round and goes out the back door and I hear the car engine start.

I run outside, chasing him. 'Dad!' I call.

Dad looks out the window. He looks me in the eye, then turns to face the driveway, and in one horrifying moment I think he's going to drive away, leave me there, soaking in my guilt and self-loathing, but he gets out of the car, walks towards me and folds me into him. I sob, loudly, snottily, and Dad pats me on the back and in a rare gesture of affection, kisses the top of my head and he leans down and whispers in my ear, 'It's OK, Bridie. It's OK, love.' He pushes me back gently and tells me to go back inside, and he gets back in the car and drives away.

I go inside. Cameron looks at me, strangely, as though he doesn't know what to think, but Mitchell walks towards me, places a hand on my shoulder, looks at me and says, very quietly, 'I'm glad you're OK, Bridie.' And he and Cameron head off up the hall to the bedroom.

I slink over to the dining room table, take a seat and bury my head in my arms. I'm so tired I can hardly see straight, and so sad and still so frightened and I thought that I would come home and see June and everything would be OK but now Dad says she's still at the hospital and Mum is there too and I don't know what it means and now I can't hold the tears back. I sob into my arms, my shoulders convulsing, my mouth drooling onto the table.

And then Debbie comes to sit beside me. She places an arm around my shoulder and I bury my face into her neck and she pats my back and she tells me, 'It's OK, It's OK, Bridie, it's going to be OK,' even though there's something there in her voice, the same thing in Dad's voice, that didn't sound entirely convinced that everything really was going to be OK.

Debbie tells Aunty Ruby to go and fix me something warm to

drink and Aunty Ruby comes back out of the kitchen with a hot Milo and a piece of toast with peanut butter and I'm not really hungry but I sip at the Milo and take a nibble at the toast and then Debbie gets up and tells me she's going to run me a hot bath.

When I've had as much Milo and toast as I can stomach, Debbie guides me into the bathroom. She helps me get undressed, tutting and shaking her head at my shredded shorts and scratched up legs and blistered feet. She helps me into the bath and I sink down into the warm, bubbly water and she takes the sponge and rubs some soap into it and she washes my back and fills the sponge with water and squeezes it over my shoulders, my head, and it feels so good.

And finally, I ask Debbie, 'What happened to June?'

Debbie tells me that on the evening before, the grown-ups noticed that June and I had been missing a long time. Mum sent Cameron outside to find us and tell us it was time to come in. Cameron did a full search around the house, the veranda, the fig tree, even the dairy shed, but when he couldn't find us, he came back in to raise the alarm. Then everyone was searching for us.

'Was it dark by that time?' I ask her.

'Yes,' she says.

I figure it must have been a long time after June's fall. I wonder how far I was up the hill, how far away I was from June, still breathing, lying in the dirt.

Debbie says everyone went in separate directions, calling our names. Then Mitchell came running out of the dairy shed, saying he'd found June. She was conscious, but still lying on the ground in Rocket-Beau's yard.

'Mitchell?' I ask, incredulous.

'Uh-huh,' she says. 'He told your dad to go call an ambulance, and he sat with June until they came.'

'Was June –' I'm not sure what I'm asking. 'Was she…was she awake?'

'Yes, but she was very groggy.'

'Did she say what happened to her?' I ask.

Debbie looks at me a while and then she says, 'She just kept saying your name.'

And my tears come afresh. 'Why is she in the hospital?' I sob. 'I mean, what's wrong with her?"

Debbie takes a long time to answer, as though she's debating how much she should tell me. 'Well, her leg is broken, pretty badly.'

I picture June's leg after falling off Rocket-Beau, twisted at an awful angle. 'Is that all?' I ask. 'A broken leg? Is that all?'

Debbie sighs, turns a shampoo bottle upside down over my head and starts to lather it in. 'She's got a head injury, we know that much. We'll have to wait and see.'

And that sick feeling slides through me. Ice water in my veins. It feels like a ferris wheel. The terror, the relief and the terror again. I don't know what to think.

When I've been in the bath so long the water is getting cold, Debbie helps me out. She wraps a towel around me and leaves me to dry myself while she brings me some clean pyjamas. I pat myself down, even splashing some of Aunty Ruby's talcum powder on my tummy. It feels good to be warm and clean.

Dressed for bed, Debbie walks me up to the bedroom. I see she's turned the bed sheets down. I crawl up into the bed and she tucks me in, even bending down to kiss my cheek.

'Get some sleep, Bridie,' she says. She pulls on the piece of string and with a loud click, the light goes out.

I want to ask her to stay, to lie down in the bed next to me, but then I hear baby Alex crying down the hall and I hear Debbie walking down the hall towards him.

I roll over, stare out the window. The lights are still on in the kitchen and I can see the outline of the fig tree. Up on the highway, I see a lone car, climbing the highway. I wonder whether it's a police car, out looking for me.

I stretch my arm out, across the place where June should be, asleep in the bed next to me. I feel a piece of hard plastic beneath my arm. It's the belly of June's horsey pillow. I push the button and a circle of horses start prancing on the ceiling. And it seems so ridiculous to me, right now, to have been jealous of a stupid toy horse. It even seems ridiculous to have been jealous of a real horse. And I think that I don't care whether I never actually own a horse in my whole life. I don't want a horse. I don't want to trot around in a stupid circle on a stupid horse.

I just want June to be OK. Please God, please. Let June be OK.

12

The light feels strange when I wake up. It's like the sun is in the wrong spot. I sit up and swing my legs around, about to get out of bed, but I feel dizzy, light-headed. I have to sit there for a moment and wait for the spots before my eyes to go away.

I walk into the hall, pop my head around my mum and dad's bedroom door. Dad isn't there, but my mum is in bed. Asleep. She's lying on her back with one arm stretched out across the bed where Dad should be. The other arm is on her belly. Her mouth is wide open, making little throaty sounds when she breathes in.

I wander down the hall, peeking into each room. Aunty Ruby and Uncle Evan's room is empty. The bedroom where Cameron and Mitchell and Debbie and the baby sleep is empty. I go into the kitchen, but no one is there. I'm shocked to see that the kitchen clock says it's almost eleven in the morning. I don't remember ever sleeping this late.

I visit the outhouse and go back up the hall to get dressed. Then I head across to the milking shed.

The concrete floor in the shed is clean. I can see little puddles from where it's been hosed down this morning but it's almost dry. I can smell the milk and the zesty tang of lucerne hay.

I cross the dairy shed and round the corner. I stop short when I see that Chelsea and Sondra are there. Chelsea, in her blue jodhpurs and shiny black boots is brushing Rocket-Beau's tail. I can see her little earrings glimmering in the sun. Sondra has her back to me, Rocket-Beau's front hoof resting in between her knees as she picks out the mud and rocks from his hoof with a hoof pick. I panic, make to turn around and leave, but as I do, Sondra drops the hoof and catches sight of me.

102

'Bridie,' she says, smiling. 'How are you?'

I'm stunned. I wait for her to say something about me putting a saddle on Rocket-Beau, about June's fall. But she just keeps smiling.

'I'm OK,' I say.

'Enjoying your holiday?' she asks.

I nod.

'You guys have been here a while now. You must be going home pretty soon, no?'

I shrug. 'We were supposed to leave yesterday, but now, I don't know what's happening.'

Sondra nods, moves to the back of the horse, taps his hind leg and the horse obediently lifts his hoof for her to wedge between her knees. I'm stunned. I can only assume that Sondra and Chelsea don't know what happened. I can only assume that Uncle Evan took the saddle off, the bridle off, and didn't tell them what happened.

I mutter a goodbye and go back inside the house. Aunty Ruby is there now, in the kitchen. She says good morning and asks if I want something to eat. I'm not hungry, but I help myself to a large glass of orange juice, and then another. And then I turn to see my mum in the kitchen doorway.

I'm frozen. The sickness waves through me. I'm scared that Mum will be angry, like Dad was. Like Cameron was. But then, my mum tilts her head to the side, opens her arms and bids me to come to her.

I almost run. I slam up against her body and wrap my arms around her so tight I almost knock her off balance. And I'm crying, so hard, and telling her I'm sorry, I'm sorry, I'm sorry, I'm sorry and she holds me and rubs her chin across the top of my head and tells me to 'ssssshhhhhh' and then she says, 'It's OK, Bridie, it was an accident.'

And the relief that washes over me turns my legs to jelly and I shake with crying and I say to her, 'Please let me stay in the family,' and my mum pushes back from me and looks at my face, my eyes, and her forehead crinkles with confusion and she says, 'What?' and I ask again that she please lets me stay in the family and she laughs. She actually laughs and she holds me again and sighs and says, 'Bridie, trust me, there is nothing, nothing, you could do that would make you not be a part of this family.'

Mum walks me over to the table and we sit down. She says good morning to Aunty Ruby, who turns the kettle on and makes mum a cup of coffee. Aunty Ruby tells us that Dad came back early this morning and now Uncle Evan and Dad have taken the boys down to the jetty for a fish and Mum nods and says, 'That's good,' and sips on her coffee and tells me to go and wash my face and brush my teeth and put some shoes on. Because we're going to visit June.

*

In the car on the way to the hospital, Mum tells me to prepare myself for seeing June.

'What do you mean?' I ask her.

And Mum tells me June's leg is plastered. She tells me she has a head injury, that her head is bandaged and that the doctors are still doing tests.

'Is she going to be OK?' I ask.

But Mum's chin quivers and she doesn't answer me.

*

The hospital is a grey brick building. Mum parks the car and we have to walk a long way across the car park to the entrance. Mum walks confidently, with purpose. She knows exactly where she's going, as though she comes here every day. We even pass a nurse in the hall who smiles at my mum and says, 'Hello, Leeanne.'

We get in a lift and travel up a couple of floors and Mum tells me this is the ward where June is. We step out of the lift and there's a terrible smell. A mixture of disinfectant and soup and maybe a faint hint of poo. When I breathe in, it seems like the smell is sticking to my tongue. There's a desk there with a couple of nurses behind it wearing matching green uniforms.

Mum goes to the desk and speaks quietly with the nurse, nodding at something the nurse is saying and then she turns to me and tells me that June's doctor wants to talk to her and I'm to stay where I am while Mum follows one of the nurses into a little room opposite the nurse's station.

I sit down on one of the cold, plastic chairs and watch a patient walking up the hall, pushing a metal pole with a plastic bag hanging off it, a tube leading into his bandaged hand. His gown hangs open at the back and I can see his saggy butt cheeks.

It takes a long while for Mum to speak to the doctor. It seems like she's in that little room forever but then she comes out, saying 'Thank you, doctor, thank you so much,' holding his hand in both of her hands and chewing on her bottom lip and she turns to me and walks towards me and her eyes are all wet and creased and she sits next to me and she holds my hand and she lets out a huge sigh and then she sobs, in a tight, thin voice, 'She's going to be all right, Bridie. The doctor says she's going to be all right.'

And we're both crying then, sitting there squeezing each other's hand and Mum shakes my hand up and down in her hand and she says, 'Let's go and see your sister.'

I walk with Mum up the hall a little way and we turn into a room that has a poster of a colourful butterfly on it. And my eyes bulge at the sight of June. There's a bandage around her hand and a tube leading up to a bag that's hanging off a metal pole, just like the one I saw with the man in the hall. Her leg is wrapped from her knee to her hip and it's propped up on a stack of pillows. Her body looks so tiny compared to the thickness of the wrapped leg. And there's a bandage around her head. I can see a bit of her hair at the top of her head but the bandage is wrapped thickly around the sides of her head, covering half of both of her ears. Her eyes are closed. And I wonder whether she's in a coma. Even though Mum said she's going to be all right, I wonder whether she's in a coma. I've heard of a coma, a deep sleep from which you can't wake up.

But then Mum moves to the side of the bed and she takes a hold of June's hand and she squeezes it and she whispers, 'June.' Again. 'June?'

And June's beautiful big blue eyes flutter open and she looks at my mum and a little smile dances across her lips. And then I move to the bed and June turns her head, slowly, towards me, and big fat tears spill over the rims of my eyes and down my cheeks and make a pat-pat sound as they hit the hard hospital sheets and June's face almost lights up and she smiles and she says, 'Bridie!' And I lean over June's body and give her a hug, careful not to touch her leg or her bandage on her head and I tell her I'm so happy to see her and I'm so sorry.

'What are you sorry for, Bridie?' June asks me. She actually asks me what I have to be sorry about and I tell her I'm sorry it was my fault she fell off Rocket-Beau and it's my fault now she's in hospital with a broken leg and a big fat bandage on her head and June says, 'Don't cry, Bridie. You didn't mean it. It was just an accident.'

13

I wake early. I've slept through the rooster's morning crow but I can see the fig tree dancing in the breeze and I can tell by the light that Uncle Evan will already be in his boots, out on the quad bike with Jess and Bell, bringing in the heifers. I don my blue jeans, trot down the hallway and slip into my boots. I visit the outhouse and then hurry over to the milking shed.

Uncle Evan smiles when he sees me and hands me a bucket of bran and pollard. I savour the smell for a moment, then set about sprinkling the cow's breakfast into the crush beneath her muzzle. She snorts, and a fine mist of bran sprays out either side of her wet nostrils. Then she lazily laps it up.

When the last cow has been milked, Uncle Evan hoses down the shed, pushing the slushy mix of dirt and cow dung to the edge of the concrete, and I watch it cascade onto the grass, a bright green, bubbly froth, like the contents of a witch's cauldron.

When we're done, we head off across the house paddock. Uncle Evan tells Jess and Bell to go to bed and they obediently scurry into their respective kennels, spinning around at the base of the drums so their heads are facing outwards. Uncle Evan leans down and clicks the clasp of their chains onto their collars and they snuggle down, their morning work complete.

I follow Uncle Evan to the chook house. He moves the house bricks that are holding the gate in place and lifts it out of the way. He takes another house brick off the lid of the garbage bin that houses the chook feed and tells me to fill an ice cream container and spread it around the dirt for the chooks to scratch and peck at.

'Any eggs this morning, Bridie?' he asks.

I lower my head and peer into the wooden chook house. I see two chooks, still nestled down in their straw beds. I take a deep breath. I stretch my hand out towards the feathery breast of the chook closest to me. Slowly my hand wavers, back and forth, as I talk myself into placing my hand beneath the clucky hen. Then, the words take shape in my mind, so clearly I can hear them. 'Quick! Go!' And I thrust my hand beneath the first chook, so swiftly she doesn't even have time to react. I feel two warm, fresh eggs and bring them out, holding them up triumphantly to show Uncle Evan.

He sees my beaming face and smiles, placing a firm, kind hand on my shoulder. 'Well done, Bridie,' he tells me.

We head inside. I hand the eggs to Aunty Ruby, who is making tea in the kitchen. My tummy growls with hunger, and I help myself to orange juice and a piece of toast and sit at the dining room table with Uncle Evan, who sips his morning coffee with the paper spread out before him. Aunty Ruby joins us, sipping her tea and making 'to do' notes in her little notebook.

My mother's voice floats down the hallway. She's busy, barking orders, telling Cameron and Mitchell to strip the sheets off their beds and take them to the laundry. I know if I stick around I'll be given a similar task, so I wolf down my breakfast, drop my glass and plate in the kitchen sink and slink out the back door.

The sun is warm on my skin but the south coast breeze is cool and fresh. I suck it down, feel my lungs swell with the energy of the ocean behind the hill.

My boots sink into the spongy earth beneath me as I set off across the yard, down the hill towards the dam. Having been milked and turned out again, the cows now start to spread across the paddock like strewn pebbles, long tongues curling around tufts of luscious grass. I walk among them, so close I hear their teeth shredding the grass blades and feel the steam rising off their coats as the warm sun heats their wet flanks.

I follow the fence line down to the dam, circle its perimeter. The water level is high after all the rain and I pick up a stone, try to skim it across the water the way I've seen Cameron do it. But the stone plunks and sinks as soon as it breaks the surface. The sound is fat. And satisfying.

I walk around the other side of the dam, cross the fence and face the hill. I wander up a little, the ascent much easier in the daylight, able to see a clear and obvious track going up through the brambles. I walk for ages, until I'm almost halfway up the hill. I turn round, survey the farm from this perspective. The roof of the house, the outhouse, the milking shed. It all seems so small and close together compared to the last time I climbed up here. I look up to the top of the hill. I could keep climbing. I could make it to the top, see and hear and taste the ocean on the other side. But my legs are tired and I know that there's no time. I sit for a moment on a boulder and catch my breath, and before long I see that Dad and Cameron and Mitchell are moving back and forth between the house and the car, packing it with our suitcases, eskies and fishing gear. I look across the hill and see the highway snaking homeward. And I know I need to move.

I walk back down the hill and return to the dairy shed for one final visit. I cross the wet, concrete floor, round the corner and go to Rocket-Beau's yard.

Rocket-Beau is standing at the fence and raises his head and pins his ears back for a moment when he notices me. I pick a bunch of grass, walk up to him, stretch out my hand and let him nuzzle at the offering. I look into his eyes, brown and deep, framed with those long lashes. I search there for some sort of acknowledgment, some sign of connection with me. I'm looking for an apology. I want to see him show some sadness, some shame for hurting June. But he just rips another bunch of grass from my hand, nodding his head up and down as he chews. There's nothing. There's nothing there at all. And I scratch him behind the ears and rub him on the front of his dopey face.

I leave the dairy shed and go past Jess and Bell, each lying down sleepily inside their kennels now. Although a huge tree shades them from the strengthening morning sun, their tongues loll and they look up and start to pant as I approach. After making sure Uncle Evan can't see me through the kitchen window, I bend down and pat Jess, massaging one of her velvety ears and she pushes into me, groaning a little with the pleasure of a massage. I reach across and scratch Bell underneath the chin and she rolls on her side, lifting up one leg, imploring a tummy rub. And I sit between their kennels, giving one dopey dog an ear massage and the other a tummy rub.

I make my way across the grass, cut through the brood of chooks and over to the fig tree. I hug one of the low branches and swing my legs up and over, letting go of my arms and hanging upside down. Soon, the blood rushes to my head and my face throbs. I plant my feet on the ground and run my hand across the trunk of the tree, across the names, Peter, Debbie, Cameron, and now Bridie. And I decide it's stupid that Cameron says you need to wait until you can write your name yourself. I hunt around the base of a tree, looking for a sharp rock, and around about the height I guess that June's eyes would be, I scratch her name into the bark, struggling to keep the letters soft and round. It's awkward and jagged, but it's there, in amongst our names now. June.

Finally, I'm back at the house. I sense the strange energy that runs between people about to leave each other.

'Where have you been?' Mum scolds.

Aunty Ruby is packing sandwiches and slices and insisting that Mum takes the last of the potato salad while mum tries, vainly, to refuse. Dad is double checking the fishing tackle, making sure all the rods have been collected and Mum instructs me to go look under the bed for stray socks and toothbrushes. Everyone is sort of bumping into each other and muttering 'sorry' and 'excuse me', and eventually we're all standing awkwardly around the car as Dad lights a cigarette and says, quite unnecessarily, 'Well, I think that's it then.'

Uncle Evan shakes Dad's hand, then Cameron's and lastly, Mitchell's, whose hand he takes with both his own and holds for just a beat longer, meeting his eyes with something like gratitude or respect, and I'm hit with a tirade of complicated feelings. There's more hugging and utterings of 'goodbye' and 'drive safely' and 'see you next time' and everyone piles into the car.

Dad is in the driver's seat, cigarette dangling out the corner of his mouth, hands firmly wrapped around the wheel. Mum is resting her arm along the lip of the window, waving goodbye with the other hand, her huge sunglasses covering half her face. Cameron is in the back next to the right window, Mitchell nestled in beside him. And I'm next to Mitchell.

The car picks up speed as we head down the driveway. At the bottom of the driveway, I jump out to open the gate, swinging on it as I do, waiting for the Valiant to drive through and hitching the gate closed behind it. I give one last glance back towards Samantha's house. This is the first time I've gone back home from our south coast holiday without spending any time with Samantha. And somehow, it doesn't matter now. I clamber back into my seat beside Mitchell and we enter the bitumen.

Before long, there's a warm sensation tickling the palm of my hand. I look down to find a palm pressed against mine, fingers intertwined around my own.

It's June. June has taken hold of my hand and she leans her head on my shoulder, the bandage wrapped around her skull rubbing on my bare skin. I move across the seat a little closer to Mitchell to make room for June's plastered leg. And I give her hand a little squeeze.

As we hit the highway, I watch the countryside fall away behind us, fenced off paddocks dotted with cattle and horses like patchwork tapestries in Mum's rear-view mirror. And I settle in for the long drive.

The long drive home.

www.ingramcontent.com/pod-product-compliance
Lightning Source LLC
Chambersburg PA
CBHW051233210726
48290CB00003B/934